A Text Book Of

ADVANCED WEB TECHNOLOGIES

For

BBA (Computer Application) Formerly known as BCA

Semester - VI

As Per Revised Syllabus Effective from June 2015

Mr. A. B. Nimbalkar

M.C.S. M.Phil
Sr. Lecturer in Dept. of Computer Science
PDEA's Annasaheb Magar College,
Hadapsar, Pune.

Mrs. Shalaka R. Sakhrekar

M.C.S., M.C.A., M.B.A., M.P.M.
Assistant Professor,
Sinhgad School of Business Management,
Ambegaon (Bk), Pune.

NIRALI PRAKASHAN
ADVANCEMENT OF KNOWLEDGE

N3472

BCA – VI : ADVANCED WEB TECHNOLOGIES   **ISBN 978-93-5164-851-2**

Second Edition :   January, 2017

©   :   **Authors**

Published By :
NIRALI PRAKASHAN
Abhyudaya Pragati, 1312, Shivaji Nagar,
Off J.M. Road, PUNE – 411005
Tel - (020) 25512336/37/39, Fax - (020) 25511379
Email : niralipune@pragationline.com

DISTRIBUTION CENTRES

PUNE

Nirali Prakashan	:	119, Budhwar Peth, Jogeshwari Mandir Lane, Pune 411002, Maharashtra
		Tel : (020) 2445 2044, 66022708, Fax : (020) 2445 1538
		Email : bookorder@pragationline.com, niralilocal@pragationline.com
Nirali Prakashan	:	S. No. 28/27, Dhyari, Near Pari Company, Pune 411041
		Tel : (020) 24690204 Fax : (020) 24690316
		Email : dhyari@pragationline.com, bookorder@pragationline.com

MUMBAI

Nirali Prakashan	:	385, S.V.P. Road, Rasdhara Co-op. Hsg. Society Ltd.,
		Girgaum, Mumbai 400004, Maharashtra
		Tel : (022) 2385 6339 / 2386 9976, Fax : (022) 2386 9976
		Email : niralimumbai@pragationline.com

DISTRIBUTION BRANCHES

JALGAON

Nirali Prakashan	:	34, V. V. Golani Market, Navi Peth, Jalgaon 425001,
		Maharashtra, Tel : (0257) 222 0395, Mob : 94234 91860

KOLHAPUR

Nirali Prakashan	:	New Mahadvar Road, Kedar Plaza, 1st Floor Opp. IDBI Bank
		Kolhapur 416 012, Maharashtra. Mob : 9850046155

NAGPUR

Pratibha Book Distributors	:	Above Maratha Mandir, Shop No. 3, First Floor,
		Rani Jhanshi Square, Sitabuldi, Nagpur 440012, Maharashtra
		Tel : (0712) 254 7129

DELHI

Nirali Prakashan	:	4593/21, Basement, Aggarwal Lane 15, Ansari Road, Daryaganj
		Near Times of India Building, New Delhi 110002
		Mob : 08505972553

BENGALURU

Pragati Book House	:	House No. 1, Sanjeevappa Lane, Avenue Road Cross,
		Opp. Rice Church, Bengaluru – 560002.
		Tel : (080) 64513344, 64513355,Mob : 9880582331, 9845021552
		Email:bharatsavla@yahoo.com

CHENNAI

Pragati Books	:	9/1, Montieth Road, Behind Taas Mahal, Egmore,
		Chennai 600008 Tamil Nadu, Tel : (044) 6518 3535,
		Mob : 94440 01782 / 98450 21552 / 98805 82331,
		Email : bharatsavla@yahoo.com

niralipune@pragationline.com | www.pragationline.com

Also find us on   www.facebook.com/niralibooks

Preface ...

I take this opportunity to present this book entitled as **"Advanced Web Technologies"** to the students of B.B.A. (Computer Application) Semester VI. The object of this book is to present the subject matter in a most concise and simple manner. The book is written strictly according to the Revised Syllabus of the University.

The book has its own unique features. It brings out the subject in a very simple and lucid manner for easy and comprehensive understanding of the basic concepts, its intricacies, procedures and practices. This book will help the readers to have a broader view on Advanced Web Technologies Concepts. The language used in this book is easy and will help students to improve their vocabulary of Technical terms and understand the matter in a better and happier way.

I sincerely thank Shri. Dineshbhai Furia and Shri. Jignesh Furia of Nirali Prakashan, for the confidence reposed in me and giving me this opportunity to reach out to the students of BCA.

I thank Mrs. Anita Panajkar and Mrs. Aabha Athavale for their important inputs time to time and Mr. Ilyas Shaikh, Ms. Chaitali Takle who painstakingly attended to all the details to make this book appear good.

I also thank Mr. Ravindra Walodare, Mr. Sachin Shinde, Nikunj Joshi, Nilesh Deshmukh, Ashok Bodke, Moshin Sayyed and Nitin Thorat.

I have given my best inputs for this book. Any suggestions towards the improvement of this book and sincere comments are most welcome on niralipune@pragationline.com.

AUTHORS

Syllabus ...

☞ ☞ ☞

Contents ...

Chapter 1...

Introduction to Object Oriented Programming in PHP

Contents ...

1.1 Introduction

This chapter deals with various Object Oriented concepts, and use of those concepts in PHP.

Object oriented programming (OOP) was first introduced in PHP4. Area for OOP in PHP version 4 was not very vast. There were only few features available in PHP4. Major concept of the object oriented programming in PHP is introduced from version 5 (commonly known as PHP 5). Also PHP community has plan to modify its object model structure in more better manner in PHP6. But still in PHP5 object model is designed nicely.

1.2 Classes

Class is a blueprint of any object in OOP and it is an actual code that defines the properties and methods. A class describes the characteristics and behaviour of all the members of a set. In OOP, characteristics of a class are known as its 'properties'. Properties have a name and a value.

Classes contain variables and functions, which are referred to as attributes (or properties) and methods. A class's attributes and methods are called its members. The methods you define within a class are defined just like functions outside of a class. They can take arguments, have default values, return values, and so on.

Attributes within classes are a little different than variables outside of classes. First, all attributes must be prefixed with a keyword indicating the variable's visibility.

The syntax to create a class is :

Declare a class using the class keyword, followed by the name of the class and a set of curly braces ({}). In class block you can define properties as class variable and function as class behavior

```
class class_name
{
    properties;
    functions()
    {
    }
}
```

So let us create a class for interest calculator and define its properties like rate, capital, duration and behavior like calculate interest.

```php
<?php
class interestCalculator
{
var $rate;
var $capital;
var $duration;

function calcInterest()
{
return ($this->rate*$this->duration*$this->capital)/100;
}
}
?>
```

Above is a very simple and basic class to calculate interest. Let us look at all basic aspect of this class. You can create class in PHP by using class keyword. Here class interestCalculator{ } is class block. You can define all of your properties and methods (behavior of class, we will use method or function instead of behavior) of class inside of the class block. All variable started with var keyword is property of the class. We can say these are variable and the functions are methods of this class. You can design own class with own variable and function.

1.3 Objects　　　　　　　　　　　　　**[April 2016, Oct. 2016]**

An object is an instance or occurrence of a class. It is a concrete entity constructed using the blue print provided by a class. Objects can be instantiated, which means we create a new object from a class.

In PHP, we can define objects in similar ways;

To instantiate an object, we make use of the '**new**' keyword.

Instantiating an object we require two things :

1. **A memory location** into which the objects are loaded.
2. **The data** that will populate the value or state.

Once you defined your class, then you can create as many objects as you like of that class type. Following is an example which shows how to create object of class by using 'new' operator.

Syntax for creating an object :

```
<? php
    $calculator = new interestcalculator( );
?>
```

A class never has property values or state, only objects can.

Classes are manipulated at design-time, when you make changes to the methods or properties and objects are manipulated at runtime when values are assigned to their properties and their methods are invoked.

The '$this' Variable: '$this' is available when a method is called from within an object context. $this is a reference to the calling object (usually the object to which the method belongs, but possibly another object, if the method is called statically from the context of a secondary object).

For example:

$this->getName();

Method: In OOP, a method is a function within a class. Use methods in the exact way as you would normally use a function. You can pass arguments into the method if you wish.

Delcaring A Method

```
funtion getName(){
// code here
}
```

To call the method, use the object variable, as well as -> followed by the method name.

But to call a method from outside a class, you have to first create an object of the class and then use the object to call the method:

Example 1:

$calculator = new InterestCalculator()

$calculator -> rate = 3;

$calculator -> duration = 2;

$calculator -> capital = 300;

echo $calculator -> calculateInterest();

Example 2:

$objTest = new Test( );

$objTest → name = 'PHP';

$objTest → sayHello( );

The string Hello PHP ! print to the screen

Visibility: Visibility means Protecting Access to Member Variables

There are three different levels of visibility that a member variable or method can have : public, private and protected.

1. Public members are accessible to any and all code.
2. Private members are only accessible to the class itself.
3. Protected members are available to class itself and to classes that inherited from it.

Public is the default visibility level.

For example:

```
public function getName(){
// code here
}
```

Constructor of Classes and Objects:

The constructor is a special built-in method, added with PHP 5, allows developers to declare for classes. This allows to initialize object properties (i.e. the values of properties) when a object is created. Classes which have a constructor method execute automatically when an object is created. The 'construct' method starts with two underscores (_ _).

Constructor is not required if you don't want to pass any property values or perform any actions when the object is created. PHP only ever calls one constructor.

Destructor:

A destructor is a special function of a class that is automatically executed whenever an object of a class is destroyed.

An object of a class is destroyed when

1. it goes out of scope,
2. when you specifically set it to null,
3. when you unset it or when the program execution is over.

In simple terms, A destructor function is called when the object is destroyed.

A PHP5 destructor is defined by implementing the _ _destruct() method. In PHP4 however, the concept of a destructor did not exist. A destructor cannot take any arguments.

The Destructor Method is created with the _ _destruct() name which start with two undescores(_ _). It's the opposite of __construct().You have seen that the __construct() method is automatically invoked when an object is instantiated. The _ _destruct() method is automatically invoked just before the object is removed from memory (with unset($object)). This method is useful when you want to perform any last-minute actions (such as saving or printing some data when it is deleted). Destructor is the counterpart of constructor.

The general syntax for destructor declaration follows :

```
function _ _destruct ( )
{
/* Class initialization code */
}
$obj = new ClassName();
unset($obj); // Calls destructor, too.

<?php
//Define a class
class MyClass {
     function _ _construct()
{  echo 'webtechnology'.' <br>';
   $this->name = "MyClass";
}

   function _ _destruct()
   {
   print "Destroying " . $this->name . "<br>";
   }
}
$obj = new MyClass();
?>
```

Output:

Webtechnology

Destroying MyClass

Scope resolution operator(::)

In PHP, the scope resolution operator is also called Paamayim Nekudotayim which means "double colon" or "double dot twice" in Hebrew. The double colon (::), is a token which allows access to static, constant, and overridden properties or methods of a class.

Class Constants

A constant is somewhat like a variable, in that it holds a value, but is really more like a function because a constant is immutable. Once you declare a constant, it does not change. Constant names are not preceded by a dollar sign ($) like a normal variable declaration. Interfaces may also include constants. Constants are defined by using the define() function or by using the const keyword outside a class definition as of PHP 5.3.0.

When calling a class constant using the $classname :: constant syntax, the classname can actually be a variable. As of PHP 5.3, you can access a static class constant using a variable reference (Example: className :: $varConstant).

Declaring one constant is easy, as is done in this version of MyClass –

```
class MyClass
{

    const Margin = 2.5;


    function _ _construct($inValue)
    {
       // Statements here run every time
       // an instance of the class
       // is created.
    }

}
```

In this class, Margin is a constant. It is declared with the keyword const, and under no circumstances can it be changed to anything other than 2.5. Note that the constant's name does not have a leading $, as variable names do.

Define a Constant:

The name of the constant and the value must be placed within the parentheses. After defining it can never be changed or undefined. Only scalar data i.e. boolean, integer, float and string can be contained in constants.

```
<?php
define("COUNTRY_NAME", "India");
echo COUNTRY_NAME;
?>
```

Output :

India

Let us see difference between CONSTANTS and PHP Class Definitions.

Using "define('MY_VAR', 'default value')" INSIDE a class definition does not work. You have to use the PHP keyword 'const' and initialize it with a scalar value -- boolean, int, float, or string (no array or other object types) -- right away.

```
<?php
define('MIN_VALUE', '0.0');   // RIGHT - Works OUTSIDE of a class definition.
define('MAX_VALUE', '1.0');   // RIGHT - Works OUTSIDE of a class definition.
//const MIN_VALUE = 0.0;        WRONG - Works INSIDE of a class definition.
//const MAX_VALUE = 1.0;        WRONG - Works INSIDE of a class definition.
```

Class Constants

```
{
//define('MIN_VALUE', '0.0');  WRONG - Works OUTSIDE of a class definition.
//define('MAX_VALUE', '1.0');  WRONG - Works OUTSIDE of a class definition.

const MIN_VALUE = 0.0;       // RIGHT - Works INSIDE of a class definition.
const MAX_VALUE = 1.0;       // RIGHT - Works INSIDE of a class definition.
public static function getMinValue()
{
    return self::MIN_VALUE;
}

    public static function getMaxValue()
{
    return self::MAX_VALUE;
}
}
?>
```

Abstract Classes

PHP also supports class and method abstraction. An abstract class is one that cannot be instantiated, only inherited. When inheriting from an abstract class, all methods marked abstract in the parent's class declaration must be defined by the child; additionally, these methods must be defined with the same visibility. A class containing abstract Methods is called abstract class.

You can declare an abstract class with the keyword abstract like this—

```
abstract class MyAbstractClass {
    abstract function myAbstractFunction() {
    }
}
```

Note that function definitions inside an abstract class must also be preceded by the keyword abstract. It is not legal to have abstract function definitions inside a non-abstract class.

1.4 Introspection   [April 2016]

Introspection is the ability of a program to examine an object's characteristics, such as its name, parent class (if any), properties and methods. Introspection allows you to :

- Obtain the name of the class to which an object belongs as well as its member properties and methods.
- Write generic debuggers, serializers, profilers etc.

Examining Classes

The introspective functions provided by PHP are :

- **Class_exists( ) :** To determine whether a class exists, which takes in a string and returns a Boolean value. Alternately, you can use the get_declared_classes( ) function which returns an array of defined classes and checks if the class name is in the returned array.

  For example : $yes_no = class_exists(Test);

     $classes=get_declared_classes();

- **get_class_methods( ) :** Returns an array of class methods name.

  For example, $methods = get_class_methods (Test).

- **get_class_vars( ) :** Returns an array of default properties of the class.

  For example : $prop = get_classvar(Test);

- **get_class( ) :** Returns the name of the class of an object.

- **get_object_vars( ) :** Returns an associative array of object and properties.

- **get_parent_class( ) :** Retrives the parent class name for object or class.

- **is_object :** Returns true if it is an object else false.

  For example : $yes_no = is_object(var);

- **is_subclass_of( ) :** Returns true if the object has this class as one of its parents.

- **method_exist( ) :** Checks if the class method exists.

The following program will display all currently declared classes and the methods and properties for each.

```
function display_classes( )
  {
     $classes = get_declared_classes( );
     foreach ($classes as $cls)
       {
          echo "Display information of $cls";
          echo "$class methods : <br>";
          $methods = get_class_methods($cls);
          if(count($methods))
            {
               foreach($methods as $md)
               {
                  echo "$md";
               }
            }
          echo "$class properties : <br>";
```

```php
        $properties = get_class_vars($cls);
           if(count($properties))
           {
                foreach(array_keys($properties) as $prop)
                {
                    echo "$prop <br>";
                }
           }
        }
    }
```

Examining the object: To examine the object, first we will check whether it is an object. If it is a object then we will check to which class it belongs to :

```php
    $res = is_object(var);
    $classname = get_class(object_name);
    $obj_ary = get_object_vars(object_name);
```

The get_class_vars( ) returns only those properties with default values, and the get_object_vars( ) returns only those properties that are set.

```php
    <? php
    class student
        {
            var $name;
            var $age;
        }
    $ s1 = new student;
    $ s1 -> $name = 'Akash';
    $prop = get_object_vars($s1);
    ?>
    //Here prop is an array ('name' ⇒ 'fred');
```

The get_parent_class( ) function actually accept either an object or class name. It returns the name of the parent class, or false if there is no parent class.

```php
    <? php
    class Base
        {
        }
    class Derived extends Base
        {
        }
```

```
    $ Dobj = new Derived;
    echo get_parent_class ($Dobj);     // print Base
    echo get_parent_class (Derived);   // print Base
?>
```

To check if an object is an instance of a particular class or if it implements a particular interface you can use the instance of operator.

For example,

```
if ($obj instanceof Base)
    {
        echo "Base class object";
    }
```

1.5 Serialization   [Oct. 2016]

The next OOP topic is how to convert an object to a string, and vice-versa. This can be useful when you need to pass object data as strings of text between scripts and applications. Common situations include:

- Passing objects via fields in web forms
- Passing objects in URL query strings
- Storing object data in a text file, or in a single database field

To convert an object to a string — and back again — use the following PHP functions:

- serialize() takes an object, and outputs a string representation of the object's class and properties.
- unserialize() takes a string created by serialize(), and converts it back into a usable object.

Serializing an object means converting it to a byte stream representation that can be stored into a file. This is useful for permanent data. In PHP, serialization is mostly automatic.

For example,

        $ encode = serialize (somedata);

It returns a string containing a byte_stream representation.

        $ somedata = unserialize (encode);

While saving an object, all the variables of the object will be saved, but the functions will not be saved.

To unserialize( ) an object, the class must be defined. If $a object of class A, first PHP file has to be serialized then all the values of variables contained in $a and the class name is stored. If you want to unserialize it in second PHP file then the definition of class A should be present in second php file. This can be done by include file.

For example,

```
include('obj_definition.inc');  // load obj definitions
```

Consider the following example (sample.inc);

```
<? PHP
    class Student
        {
            var $age = 10;
            function show_Age ( )
                {
                    echo $this -> age
                }
        }
?>
```

The first PHP file :

```
include ('sample.inc');
$stud = new Student;
    $sri_obj = serialize ($stud);
    $fp = fopen ($file1, "w");
    fwrite ($fp, $sri_obj)'  // storing serialized obj into the file
        fclose ($fp);
```

The second PHP file :

```
include ('sample.inc');
$sr_obj = implode (" ", @file ('file1'));
$us_obj = unserailize ($sr_obj);
$us_obj -> show_Age ( );
```

The functions sleep( ) and wakeup( ) : These functions are used to notify objects that they are being serialized or unserialised. The sleep( ) method is called on an object just before serialization. It cleans up the object i.e. it closes any database connections that object may have, writing out unsaved persistent data and so on. It returns the array with the names of all variables of that object. If you return an empty array, no data is written. The wakeup( ) method is called on an object immediately after an object is created from a bytestream. It reconstruct the resources that object may have i.e. to re-establish any database connections that may be lost during serialization and perform the reinitialisation tasks.

1.6 Inheritance

The new class can inherit the properties and methods from the old class. The old class is the base class and the new class is the derived class. The derived class has its own variables and methods in addition to variables and methods from the base class. The 'extends' keyword is used for the inheritance.

Example :

```
class Person;
    {
        var $name, $age;
    }
class Employee extends Person
    {
        var $salary, $designation;
    }
```

where Person is the base class and Employee is the derived class.

The employee class contains the $salary, $designation, as well as the $name and $age properties inherited from the person class.

An extended class is always dependent on the single base class, multiple inheritance is not supported.

You can create object of Employee class.

    $obj_emp = new Employee;

Then obj_emp -> name, obj_emp -> age, obj_emp -> salary : is allowed.

Create object of person class.

    $obj_per = new Person;

    $obj_per -> name, obj_per -> age : is allowed.

    $obj_per -> salary : is not allowed.

If the derived class is having the same method name as the base class then the method in the derived class takes precedence over, or overrides the base class.

PHP does not provide for automatic chain of constructor. Only constructor in the derived class is automatically called.

Example :

```
<? php
class Base
    {
        function Base( )
```

```php
        {
            echo "Base class constructor";
        }
    }
class Derived extends Base
    {
        function Derived( )
            {
                echo "Derived class constructor";
                $this -> Base( );
            }
    }
$obj_Driv = new Derived;
?>
```

For the constructor of Base class to be called, the constructor in the Derived class must explicitly call the constructor.

The scope resolution operator (: :) is used to refer functions and variables in base class or to refer functions in classes that have not yet any instances.

Example :

```php
<? php
    class A
        {
            function show( )
                {
                    echo "The function of the base class";
                }
        }
    class B extends A
        {
            function show( )
                {
                    echo "The function of derived class";
                    A :: show( );   // The base class show( ) is called
                }
        }
    A :: sample( );    // Output : The function of the base class
```

```
$ob = new B;
$ob -> show( );// Output : The function of derived class
            // The function of base class.
```

In this example, no object of class A is created; but still you are able to call the method of class A.

In this example, override inherited show( ) method. Override a method in subclass when the parent class's implementation is different from that required by the subclass. This enables you to specialize the activities of that subclass.

PHP does not raise an error if the number of parameters passed to a user-defined function is greater than the number of parameters established in the function declaration.

References work inside the constructor, consider the following example.

```php
< ? php
class A
{
    function A($v)
        {
            $this->value=$v;
            $this->b=new Der($this);
        }
    function create_ref( )
        {
            $this->c = new Der($this);
        }
    function echov( )
        {
            echo "<br>"."class".get_class($this)." : ".$this->value;
        }
}
class Der
    {
    function Der (&$a)
        {
        $this->a= &$a;
        }
    function echovalue( )
        {
            echo "<br>"."class.get_class($this)." : ".$this->a->value;
        }
```

```
}
$a= new A(10);
$a->create_ref( );
$a->echov( );
$a->b->echovalue( );
$a->c-echovalue( );
$a->value = 11;
$a->echov( );
$a->b->echovalue( );
$a->c->echovalue( );
?>
/* Output
classA : 10
classDer : 10
classDer : 10
classA : 11
classDer : 11
classDer : 11
*/
```

1.7 Interfaces   [Oct. 2016]

Interface is a class with no data members and contains only member functions. It provides methods to implement. Any class that inherits from an interface must implement member function body. Interface is also an abstract class because abstract class always require an implementation. Interfaces may declare only methods not any variables. To extend from an Interface, keyword 'implements' is used. Derived classes may implement more than one interface. It may inherit from other interfaces using the 'extends' keyword. All methods are assumed to be public in the interface definition, can be defined explicitly as public or implicitly. When a class implements multiple interfaces there cannot be any naming collision between methods defined in the different interfaces.

Syntax:

```
interface interfacename
{
    function name( );
    function name1( );
}
```

```
class temp implements interfacename
{
   public function name
   {
   }
}
```

Example :

```
<?
interface employee
{
   function setdata($empname, $empage);
   function outputData( );
}
class Payment implements employee
{
   function setdata($empname, $empage)
   {
      // Functionality
   }
   function outputData( )
   {
      echo "Inside Payment Class";
   }
}
$a = new Payment( );
$a ->outputData( );
? >
```

Multiple Interface Inheritance :

```
<? php
interface A
{
   public function fun1( );
}
interface B
{
   public function fun2( );
}
```

```
interface C extends A, B
{
   public function fun3( );
}
class D implements C
{
   public function fun1( )
   {
      :
      :
   }
   public function fun2( )
   {
      :
      :
   }
   public function fun3( )
   {
      :
      :
   }
}
?>
```

Note : A class cannot implement two interfaces that share function names. Since it would cause ambiguity.

Combining Abstract Class and Interface Class :

```
<?
interface employee
{
   function setdata($empname, $empage);
   function outputData( );
}
abstract class Payment implements employee
        // implementing employee
        // interface
```

```php
    {
        abstract function PaymentInfo( );
    }
    class PaySlip extends Payment
    {
        function collectPaySlip( )
        {
            echo "PaySlip Collected";
            $this->outputData( );
        }
        function outputData( )
        {
            echo "Inside PaySlip Class";
        }
        function PaymentInfo( )
        {
            echo "Inside PaySlip Class";
        }
        function setData($empname, $empage)
        {
            //  Functionality
        }
    }
    $a = new PaySlip( );
    $a->collectPaySlip( );
    ?>
```

Output :

```
PaySlip Collected
Inside Payment Class
```

1.8 Encapsulation

The ability to hide the details of implementation is known as encapsulation. The encapsulation is used for protection of a class's internal data from code outside that class, and hiding the details of implementation.

The main advantage of encapsulation is that, you can change the implementation details at any time without affecting code that uses your class. It hides the complexity and makes system easier to maintain.

Encapsulation means, visibility. It refers to visibility of methods or properties of a class. There are three types of visibilities like public, private and protected. We use these to decide that whether our methods or properties are going to use child class or within class.

Sometimes, it is needed to make sure that properties are only usable in own class. In this case, we have to use encapsulation prefix. Let's consider a class where we have to store users name, social security id and how much tax he or she have to pay. In this situation, we use following keywords for visibility.

Public: The method is publicly available and can be accessed by all subclasses.

Protected: The method / function / property is available to the parent class and all inheriting classes or we call them subclasses or child classes.

Private: The method is private and only available to the parent class / base class.

You cannot access your private or protected properties directly from outside of your class but you can use through any methods.

Let's take a look,

Class Encap

```
{
    /**
     * [$name Store name of the users. It is public and can be called in
same class as well as child class]
     * @var String
     */
    public $name;
    /**
     * [$id Keep social secirty numbers that are private. Only call in
same class]
     * @var Integer
     */
    private $id;
    /**
     * [$tax It is protected and only used on child class ]
     * @var Float
     */
    protected $tax;
    /**
     * [userId This is a public method where we can access private or
protected properties from outside of this class.]
```

```
    *  @return  integer  returning  a  private  or  protected  variable  to
public
    */
   public function userId()
   {
      return $this->id = 456;
   }
}
 $obj = new Encap();
echo $obj->userId();
```

It is highly recommended to use_(underscore) as a prefix of private properties or methods. It reminds that anything start with _ meaning that it is private properties or methods. In nutshell, encapsulation refers to visibility level of methods or properties in programming code. Simply it sensitized the access level of class staff that are highly needed.

Practice Questions

1. What is OOP in PHP?
2. How to create an object in PHP?
3. What is inheritance? Explain with suitable example?
4. What is the use of constants in OOP ?
5. Define the concept of encapsulation with example.
6. Define following terms: Introspection, serialization
7. How will create interfaces in OOP code?
8. What is meant by the term visibility of methods?
9. Write the difference between constructor and destructor methods.
10. What is meant by an abstract class?

✍ ✍ ✍

Chapter **2**...

Web Techniques

Contents ...

2.1 Introduction

PHP was designed as a web scripting language and, although it is possible to use it in purely command-line and GUI scripts, the Web accounts for the vast majority of PHP uses. In this chapter, you will learn how PHP provides access to form parameters and uploaded files, how to send cookies and redirect the browser, how to use PHP sessions, and more.

The web runs on HTTP (Hyper Text Transfer Protocol). This protocol governs how web browsers request files from web servers and how the servers send the files back.

When a web browser requests a web page, it sends an HTTP request message to a web server. The request message always includes some header information, and it sometimes also includes a body. The web server responds with a reply message, which always includes header information and usually contains a body. The first line of an HTTP request looks like this:

```
GET /index.html HTTP/1.1
```

This line specifies an HTTP command, called a method, followed by the address of a document and the version of the HTTP protocol being used. In this case, the request is using the GET method to ask for the index.html document using HTTP 1.1. After this initial line, the request can contain optional header information that gives the server additional data about the request. For example:

```
User-Agent: Mozilla/5.0 (Windows 2000; U) Opera 6.0 [en]
Accept: image/gif, image/jpeg, text/*, */*
```

The User-Agent header provides information about the web browser, while the Accept header specifies the MIME types that the browser accepts. After any headers, the request contains a blank line, to indicate the end of the header section. The request can also contain additional data, if that is appropriate for the method being used (e.g., with the POST method, as we'll discuss shortly). If the request doesn't contain any data, it ends with a blank line.

The web server receives the request, processes it, and sends a response. The first line of an HTTP response looks like this:

```
HTTP/1.1 200 OK
```

This line specifies the protocol version, a status code, and a description of that code. In this case, the status code is "200", meaning that the request was successful (hence the description "OK"). After the status line, the response contains headers that give the client additional information about the response. For example:

```
Date: Fri, 26 Jan 2015 20:25:12 GMT
Server: Apache 1.3.22 (Unix) mod_perl/1.26 PHP/4.1.0
Content-Type: text/html
Content-Length: 141
```

The Server header provides information about the web server software, while the Content-Type header specifies the MIME type of the data included in the response. After the headers, the response contains a blank line, followed by the requested data, if the request was successful.

The two most common HTTP methods are GET and POST. The GET method is designed for retrieving information, such as a document, an image, or the results of a database query from the server. The POST method is used for posting information, such as a credit-card number or information that is to be stored in a database, to the server. The GET method is what a web browser uses when the user types in a URL or clicks on a link. When the user submits a form, either the GET or POST method can be used, as specified by the method attribute of the form tag.

2.2 Web Variables   [Oct. 2016]

The PHP script must communicate with the outside world. The PHP scripts sends the data to the browser and collect data from the same. From the outside world, the input generally comes from HTML forms. These fields of the form are turned into the variables. When the URL (Uniform Resource Locater) is specified in the browser then the first task of the browser is to break it into parts. The first part is the protocol HTTP (Hyper Text Transfer Protocol).

Next is the name of the web server to which the browser makes a connection. The browser identifies the document it wants from the web server and it is done using HTTP protocol. The browser may provide some extra lines of information called headers.

The web server places these headers into environment variables to conform with CGI (Common Gateway Interface). The header is sent by the browser as user-agent. The web server creates an environment variable called **HTTP_USER_AGENT**.

PHP creates a separate global variable for every form parameter. Several predefined variables in PHP are "superglobals", which means that they are always accessible, regardless of scope - and you can access them from any function, class or file without having to do anything special. Regardless of the setting of register-globals, PHP creates six global arrays that contain the EGPCS information (Environment, GET, POST, Cookies and Server). The global variables are also visible within function definition. The global arrays are :

$GLOBALS: $GLOBALS is a PHP super global variable which is used to access global variables from anywhere in the PHP script (also from within functions or methods).

$_COOKIE: Contains any cookie values passed as part of the request ($HTTP_COOKIE_VARS).

$_REQUEST: PHP $_REQUEST is used to collect data after submitting an HTML form.

$_GET : Contain any parameters that are part of a GET request.

$_POST : Contains any parameters that are part of a POST request.

$_FILES : Contains information about any uploaded files ($HTTP_POST_ FILES).

$_SERVER : Contain useful information about the web server.

$_ENV : Contains The values of any environment variable.

$_SESSION: contains user information to be used across multiple pages (e.g. username, favorite color, etc)

PHP automatically create the $_REQUEST array, which contains the element of the $_GET, $_POST and $_COOKIE arrays all in one array variable.

PHP also creates a variable called $PHP_SELF, which holds the name of the current script. This value is also accessible as $_SERVER['PHP_SELF'].

PHP $GLOBALS: $GLOBALS is a PHP super global variable which is used to access global variables from anywhere in the PHP script (also from within functions or methods). PHP stores all global variables in an array called $GLOBALS[index]. The index holds the name of the variable.

The example below shows how to use the super global variable $GLOBALS:

Example

```php
<?php
$a = 80;
$b = 20;
function addition()
{
    $GLOBALS['c'] = $GLOBALS['a'] + $GLOBALS['b'];
}
```

```
addition();
echo $c;
?>
```
Output:
```
100
```
In the above example, since c is a variable present within the $GLOBALS array, it is also accessible from outside the function.

PHP $_SERVER - [April 2016, Oct. 2016]: $_SERVER is a PHP super global variable which holds information about headers, paths, and script locations.

The example below shows how to use some of the elements in $_SERVER:

Example
```
<?php
echo $_SERVER['PHP_SELF'];
echo "<br>";
echo $_SERVER['SERVER_NAME'];
echo "<br>";
echo $_SERVER['HTTP_HOST'];
echo "<br>";
echo $_SERVER['HTTP_REFERER'];
echo "<br>";
echo $_SERVER['HTTP_USER_AGENT'];
echo "<br>";
echo $_SERVER['SCRIPT_NAME'];
?>
```
Output:
```
/php/demo_global_server.php
www.pragati.com
www.pragati.com
http://www.pragati.com/php/showphp.asp?filename=demo_global_server
Mozilla/5.0 (Windows NT 6.1) AppleWebKit/537.36 (KHTML, like Gecko)
Chrome/45.0.2454.85
Safari/537.36
/php/demo_global_server.php
```

PHP $_REQUEST

The example below shows a form with an input field and a submit button. When a user submits the data by clicking on "Submit" button, the form data is sent to the file specified in the action attribute of the <form> tag. In this example, we point to this file itself for processing form data. If you wish to use another PHP file to process form data, replace that with the filename of your choice. Then, we can use the super global variable $_REQUEST to collect the value of the input field:

Example:

```
<html>
<body>

<form method="post" action="<?php echo $_SERVER['PHP_SELF'];?>">
  Name: <input type="text" name="fname">
  <input type="submit">
</form>

<?php
if ($_SERVER["REQUEST_METHOD"] == "POST") {
    // collect value of input field
    $name = $_REQUEST['fname'];
    if (empty($name)) {
        echo "Name is empty";
    } else {
        echo $name;
        }
}
?>
</body>
</html>
```

Output:

Name: [   ]   [Submit]

PHP $_GET: PHP $_GET can also be used to collect form data after submitting an HTML form with method="get". $_GET can also collect data sent in the URL.

Assume we have an HTML page that contains a hyperlink with parameters:

```
<html>
<body>

<a href="test_get.php?subject=PHP&web=W3schools.com">Test$GET</a>

</body>
</html>
```

When a user clicks on the link "Test $GET", the parameters "subject" and "web" is sent to "test_get.php", and you can then access their values in "test_get.php" with $_GET.

The example below shows the code in "test_get.php":

Example
```
<html>
<body>
<?php
echo "Study " . $_GET['subject'] . " at " . $_GET['web'];
?>
</body>
</html>
```
Output:
```
Study PHP at www.pragati.com
```

2.3 Server Information   [Oct. 2016]

The $_SERVER array contains information from the web server. This information comes from the environment variables required in the CGI specification. The complete list of entries in $_SERVER come from CGI :

SERVER_SOFTWARE	:	A string that identifies the server.
SERVER_NAME	:	The host name or IP address of the server.
GATEWAY_INTERFACE	:	The version of the CGI standard.
SERVER PROTOCOL	:	The name and revision of the request protocol.
SERVER-PORT	:	The server port number to which the request was sent.
REQUEST_METHOD	:	The method the client used to fetch the document.
PATH_INFO	:	Extra path elements given by the client.
PATH_TRANSLATED	:	The value of PATH_INFO translated by the server into a filename.
SCRIPT_NAME	:	The URL path to the current page.
QUERY_STRING	:	It fetches the query strings in the URL.
REMOTE_ADDR	:	The IP address from which the user is viewing the current page.
REMOTE_HOST	:	The hostname of the machine that requested this page.
REMOTE_ADDR	:	A string containing the IP address of the machine that requested this page.
AUTH_TYPE	:	The authentication method used to protect the page.
REMOTE_USER	:	The username with which the client authenticated.
REMOTE_IDENT	:	If the server is configured to use identification check, this is the username fetched from the host that made the web request.

CONTENT_TYPE   : The content type of the information attached to queries such as PUT and POST.

CONTENT_LENGTH   : The length of the information attached to queries such as PUT and POST.

The Apache server also creates entries in the $_SERVER array for each HTTP header in the request. The two most common and useful headers are :

1. **HTTP_USER_AGENT :** The string, the browser used to identify itself.
2. **HTTP_REFERER :** To get the current page.

2.4 Self Processing Forms   [April 2016]

The form parameters are available in the $_GET and $_POST arrays.

2.4.1 Methods

There are two HTTP methods that a client can use to pass form data to the server : GET and POST.

A GET request encodes the form parameters in the URL, called a query string. The GET requests are idempotent i.e., one GET request for a particular URL. GET requests should be used only for queries. The data is exposed and can be easily traced by visiting the history pages of the browser. Any login details with password should never be passed by using GET method. There are some restrictions in size of data to be posted through URL.

A POST request passes the form parameters in the body of the HTTP request. POST requests are not idempotent. This means that they cannot be catched. POST method is used to authentic data like login and password. There are no restrictions in size of data to be posted through HTTP.

2.4.2 Parameters

The $_POST, $_GET and $_FILES array are used to access form parameters from PHP code. These arrays are associative array in which keys are parameter names and values of those parameters.

The periods in field names are converted to underscores (_) in the array.

The following example shows an HTML form that chunkifies a string accepted from user. It uses two fields, one for string and one for the size of the chunks (small part).

e.g.

```
//  chn.html
    <html>
    <head> <title> chunkify form </title>
    </head> <body>
    <form action = "chunk.php" method = "POST">
    Enter a string : <input type = "text" name = "word "/> <br/>
```

```
How long should the chunks be ?
<input type = "text" name = "size" /> <br/>
<input type = "submit" value = "Chunkify !">
</form>
</body>
</html>
```

The script copies the parameter values into variables and use them.

```
//  chunk.php
<html>
<head> <title> chunked string </title>
</head>
<body>
<? php
$word = $_POST ['word'];
$size = $_POST ['size'];
$chunks = ceil (strlen($word)/ $size);
echo "The {$size}_letter chunks of '{$word}' are : <br/> \n";
for($i=0; $i<$chunks; $i++)
{
    $cnk = substr ($word, $i*$size, $size);
    printf("%d : $s <br /> \n", $i+1, $cnk);
}
?>
</body>
</html>
```

If word of 13 char and size = 3 then chunks = 5 i.e. ceil (13/3) = ceil (4·3) = 5.

Output:

```
Enter a word = 'PuneUniversity'
How long should the chunks be ? 3.
```

Output:

The 3-letter chunks of ' PuneUniversity' are:

1 : Pun

2 : eUn

3 : ive

4 : rsi

5 : ty

2.4.3 Automatic Quoting of Parameters

The option magic_quotes_gpc enabled in php_ini. This option instructs PHP to automatically call addslahes( ) on all cookie data and GET and POST parameters to make it easy to use form parameters in database queries.

For example: If you want to use "O'Reilly" as a parameter but the actually passed value is "O\'Reilly". This is done by magic_quotes_gpc.

When you want to use stripslashes( ) on the values of $_GET, $_POST or $_COOKIES, first disable magic_quotes_gpc option in php.ini.

Example :

```
$val =  ini_get('magic_quotes_gpc')
        ? stripslashes ($_GET ['word'])
        : $_GET['word'];
```

2.4.4 Self-Processing Pages

The same PHP page can be used to generate a form and process it.

For example: The PHP page that converts temperature using GET method.

```
<html>
<head> <title> Temperature Conversion </title></head>
<body>

<?php
$fahr = $_GET ['Fahrenheit'];
if(is_null($fahr))
{
?>
<form action = "<?php echo $_SERVER ['PHP_SELF']?>" method = "GET">
    Fahrenheit temperature :
    <input type = "text" name = "Fahrenheit" /> <br/>
    <input type = "submit" value = "Convert to Celsius ? "/>
    </form>
    <? php
    }
    else
      {
          $celsius = ($fahr - 32) * 5/9;
          print("%.2fF is %.2fC", $fahr, $celsius);
      }
```

```
?>
</body>
</html>
```

Output:

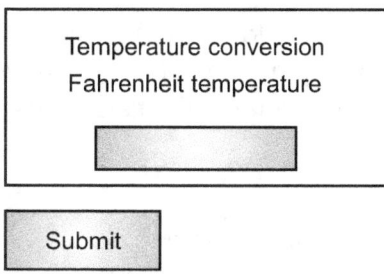

Fig. 2.1 : Output of conversion page

2.4.5 Sticky Forms   [Oct. 2016]

The results of a query are accompanied by a search form whose default values are those of the previous query is called sticky forms.

For example: In search engine, you fire any query you will get many information pages. Suppose you want some exact information then you add some words. You get some pages at top and also the result is previous query. For this basic technique is to use the submitted form value as the default value when creating the HTML field.

e.g.

```
<html>
<head> <title> Temperature conversion </title> </head>
<body>
<? php
    $f = $_GET['far'];
?>
<form action = "<?php echo $_server ['php_self]?>" method = "GET">
    Fahrenheit  temperature  :  <input  type  =  "text"  name  =
"fahrenheit" value = "/><br/>
    <input type = "submit" value = "convert" />
</form>
< ? php
    if (! is_null($f))
    {
        $c = ($f - 32) * 5/9;
        print("%.2fF is %.2fC", $f, $c);
    }
```

```
    ? >
    </body>
    </html>
```

2.4.6 Multivalued Parameters

Multiple values can be passed to a form. 'Select' tag is used for multiple selections. To ensure that PHP recognizes the multiple values that the browser passes to a form-processing script. For that you need to make the name of the field in the HTML form end with [ ].

For example:

```
<select name = "colors[ ]">
<input name = "Red"> RED </input>
<input name = "Blue"> BLUE </input>
<input name = "Yellow" > YELLOW </input>
<input name = "White" > WHITE </input>
</select>
```

Now, when user submits the form $_GET ['colors'] contains on array instead of a simple string. This array contains the values that were selected by the user.

The following example shows different colours within a HTML selection list. The user can select multiple colours his choice which will be displayed in the form.

```
<html>
<head> <title> colours </title> </head>
<body>
<form action = "<? php echo $_SERVER ['PHP_SELF']?> method = "GET">
Select your colour choices : <br/>
<select name = "colors[ ]" multiple>
<option value = "Red" > RED </option>
<option value = "Blue" > BLUE </option>
<option name = "Yellow" > YELLOW </option>
<option value = "White" > WHITE </option>
</select><br/>
<input type = "submit" name = "c" value = "Record colour choices" />
</form>
<? php   if (array_key_exists ('c', $_GET))
   {
       $desc = join (" ", $_GET['colors'];
       echo "You have a {$desc} colour choices";
   }  ?>
```

```
</body>
</html>
```

The SUBMIT button is having a name "c".

The output will be,

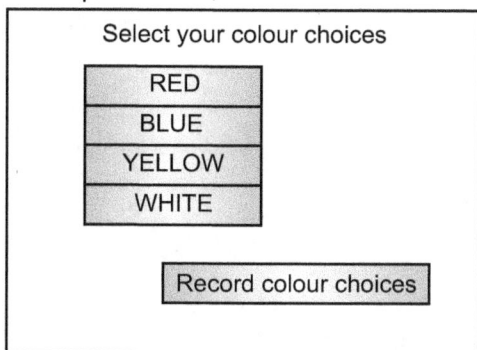
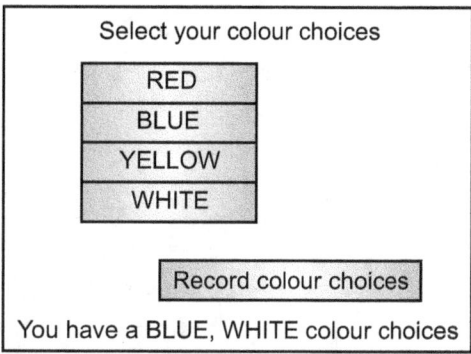

Fig. 6.2: Multiplication selection page and its output

In the same way, the form can also return multiple values.

Sticky Multivalued Parameters

You can make multiple selection form elements sticky. Here each checkbox will be checked repetitively. It's easier to write a function to generate the HTML for the possible values and work from a copy of the submitted parameters. Following example shows a new version of the multiple selection checkboxes, with the form made sticky. Although this form looks just like the previous one, behind the scenes, there are substantial changes to the way the form is generated.

For example : Multiple colours can select.using sticky multivalued parameters.

```
<html>
<head> <title> colours </title> </head>
<body>
<? php
$attr = $_GET['attributes']; // fetch from values, if any
if (!is_array ($ attr))
    {
        $attrs = array( );
    }
function make_checkboxes ($name, $query, $op)
    {
        foreach ($op as $value ⇒ $label)
        {
        printf( '%s < input type = "checkbox"
```

```
                    name = "%s[ ]" value = "%s", $label, $name, $value);
            if(in_array ($value, $query))
                {
                    echo "checked";
                }
            echo "{label}/> <br/> \n";
        }
    }
    $color_choices = array ('Red' ⇒ "RED";
                    'Blue' ⇒ "BLUE";
                    'Yellow' ⇒ "YELLOW;
                    'White' ⇒ "WHITE";
                    );
    ?>
    <form action = "<? php $_SERVER ['PHP_SELF'] ? >" method = "GET">
    select your colour choices : <br/>
    < ? php
        make_check boxes ('colors', $attrs, $color_choices);
        ? >
        <br/>
<input type = "submit" name = "c" value = "Record colour choices"/>
        </form>
        <?php if (array_key_exists ('c', $_GET))
            {
                $desc = join(" ", $_GET ['attributes']);
                echo "You have a {$desc} colour choices";
            }
            ?>
        </body>
        </html>
```

2.4.7 File Uploads   [April 2016, Oct. 2016]

To upload the file, the $_FILES array is used. Various authentication can be provided for the file uploads.

The size of the file can be limited using hard limit and a soft limit. UPLOAD_MAX_FILESIZE option in php.ini gives the hard limit to the uploaded files. If a form submits a parameter called MAX_FILE_SIZE then it is soft upper limit, the simple example is,

```
<form enctype = "multipart/form-data"
action = "<? Php echo $SERVER['PHP_SELF ']; ?>" method = "POST">
<input type = "hidden" name = "MAX_FILE_SIZE" value = "10240">
file name : <input name = "Process" $type = "file"/>
<input type = "submit" value = "Upload">
</form>
$_FILES is an array giving information about the uploaded files.
name : Name of the file
type : The MIME type of uploaded file
Size : The size of the uploaded file.
tmp_name : The name of temporary file on the server that holds the
uploaded file.
```

The uploaded files are stored in the server's default temporary files directory.

2.4.8 Form Validation

The user input data should be validated before storing it. The more secure way is to use PHP for the validation. The following example shows this where filename and caption are validated.

Example :

```
<? php
$name = $_POST['name'];
$filename = $_POST['filename'];
$caption = $_POST['caption'];
$tried = ($_POST['tried'] == 'yes');
if($tried)
    {
        $validated = (! empty($name) && ! empty ($filename));
        if(! $validated)
        {
    ?>
    <P>
    The name and filename are required fields :
    </P>
    <? php
        }
    }
```

```
if($tried && $validated)
    {
        echo '<P> The item has been created </P>';
    }
<form action = "< ? = PHP_SELF ?>" method = "POST">
Name = <input type = text name = "name"
        value = "<? = $name ?> /> <br/>
file : <input type = "text" name = "filename"
        value = "< ? = $filename ?> "/> <br/>
caption : <textarea name = "Caption">
        <? = $caption ?> </textarea> <br/>
<input type = "hidden" name = "tried" value = "yes" />
<input type = "submit"
    value = "<? PHP echo $tried ? 'continue' : 'create'; ?>" />
</form>
```

2.5 Setting Response Headers   [Oct. 2016]

The HTTP response that a server sends back to a client contains headers that identify the type of content in the body of the response, the server that sent the response, how many bytes are in the body, when the response was sent, etc. The PHP and Apache normally take care of the headers.

Before any of the body is generated, you must set the headers. The header must be top of the file.

Example :

```
<? php
header ('Content_Type : text/plain');
?>
```

2.5.1 Different Content Types

The Content_Type identifies the type of document being returned. The default are "text/html" which indicates the HTML document. The others are "text/plain" that is treat the page as a plain.text.

2.5.1.1 Redirection   [April 2016, Oct. 2016]

```
Redirection is to sent the browser to a new URL.
e.g.
    <? php
        header ('location : http://www.bgcollege.com/ index.html');
        exit ( );
        ?>
```

2.5.1.2 Expiration

A server can explicitly inform the browser, and any proxy caches that might be between the server and browser, of a specific date and time for the document to expire. Proxy and browser caches can hold the document until that time or expire it earlier. Repeated reloads of a cached document do not contact the server. However, an attempt to fetch an expired document does contact the server.

To set the expiration time of a document, use the Expires header:

```
header('Expires: Fri, 18 Jan 2020 05:30:00 GMT');
```

To expire a document three hours from the time the page was generated, use time( ) and gmstrftime( ) to generate the expiration date string:

```
$now = time( );
$then = gmstrftime("%a, %d %b %Y %H:%M:%S GMT", $now + 60*60*3);
header("Expires: $then");
```

To indicate that a document "never" expires, use the time a year from now:

```
$now = time( );
$then = gmstrftime("%a, %d %b %Y %H:%M:%S GMT", $now + 365*86440);
header("Expires: $then");
```

To mark a document as already expired, use the current time or a time in the past:

```
$then = gmstrftime("%a, %d %b %Y %H:%M:%S GMT");
header("Expires: $then");
```

2.5.1.3 Authentication

The HTTP authentication works through request headers and response status. In the request headers, a browser can send a username and password. The server can send a response.

In PHP, the PHP_AUTH_USER and PHP_AUTH_PW elements of $_SERVER are used.

The server sends a "401 Unauthorized" response and identifies the realm of authentication via www.Authenticate header.

Example :

```
header ('www-Authenticate : Basic realm="Top Secret Files" ');
header ('HTTP/1.0 401 Unauthorized");
```

The following example checks the password, which is reverse and username.

```
<? php
$user_ok = 0;
$user = $_SERVER['PHP_AUTH_USER'];
$pass = $_SERVER['PHP_AUTH_PW'];
if(isset($user) && isset($pass) && $user === strrev($pass))
```

```
    {
        $auth_ok = 1;
    }
  if(!$auth_ok)
    {
        header ('www.Authenticate : Basic realm = "Top secret" ');
        header ('HTTP/1.0 401 Unauthorized');
        // else use to see client hits 'cancel'
        exit;
    }
  ?>
  <! - You can have password-protected document here ->
```

2.6 Maintaining State (Cookies and Sessions)   [April 2016, Oct. 2016]

The state is useful for a server to recognize that a sequence of requests all originate from the same client. For maintaining state, you can use cookies and sessions.

To get around the Web's lack of state, programmers have come up with many tricks to keep track of state information between requests (also known as session tracking).

One such technique is to use hidden form fields to pass around information. PHP treats hidden form fields just like normal form fields, so the values are available in the $_GET and $_POST arrays. Using hidden form fields, you can pass around the entire contents of a shopping cart. However, a more common technique is to assign each user a unique identifier and pass the ID around using a single hidden form field. While hidden form fields work in all browsers, they work only for a sequence of dynamically generated forms, so they aren't as generally useful as some other techniques.

Another technique is URL rewriting, where every local URL on which the user might click is dynamically modified to include extra information. This extra information is often specified as a parameter in the URL. For example, if you assign every user a unique ID, you might include that ID in all URLs, as follows:

```
http://www.example.com/catalog.php?userid=123
```

If you make sure to dynamically modify all local links to include a user ID, you can now keep track of individual users in your application. URL rewriting works for all dynamically generated documents, not just forms, but actually performing the rewriting can be tedious.

A third technique for maintaining state is to use cookies. A cookie is a bit of information that the server can give to a client. On every subsequent request the client will give that information back to the server, thus identifying itself. Cookies are useful for retaining information through repeated visits by a browser, but they're not without their own problems. Let's see more about 'cookies' in next section.

Cookies

Basically, a cookie is a string that contains several fields. PHP transparently supports HTTP cookies. Cookies are mechanism for storing data in the remote browser and thus tracking or identifying return users. Cookies are part of the HTTP header.

The setcookie( ) function is used to send the cookie to the browser. The function is as follows :

```
setcookie (name[, value [, expire[, path[, domain [, secure]]]]]);
```

This function creates the cookie string from the given arguments and creates a cookie header with that string as its value. Because cookies are sent as headers in the response, setcookie( ) must be called before any of the body of the document is sent. The parameters are as follows :

name : A unique name for a particular cookie. The name must not contain whitespace or semicolons.

value : The arbitrary string value attached to this cookie.

expire : The expiration date for this cookie. If no expiration date is specified, the browser saves the cookie in the memory and not on disk. when the browser exists, the cookie disappears.

path : The browser will return the cookie only for URLs below this path.

domain : The browser will return the cookie only for URLs within this domain.

secure : The browser will transmit the cookie only over http's connections.

When a browser sends a cookie back to the server, you can access that cookie through the $_COOKIE array. The key is the cookie name, and the value is the cookie's value field.

For instance, the following code keeps track of the number of times the page has been accessed by this client :

```
<? php
$ page_access = $_COOKIE['accesses'];
setcookie ('access', ++$page_accesses);
?>
```

When decoding cookies, any periods (·) in a cookie's name are turned into underscores. For instance, a cookie named first.page is accessible as $_cookie['first.page'].

Sessions

Session support in PHP consists of a way to preserve certain data across subsequent accesses. This enables us to build more customized applications and increase the applications and also the appeal of our website. Sessions basically handle all the cookie manipulation for us to provide persistent variables which are accessible from different pages and across multiple visits.

A visitor accessing a website is assigned a unique id, called as the session-id. This stated as in a cookie on the user such as propagated in the URL.

Every session has a data store associated with it. You can register variables to be loaded from the data store when each page starts and saved back to the data store when the page ends.

Session basics : An overview of PHP session management is shown below.

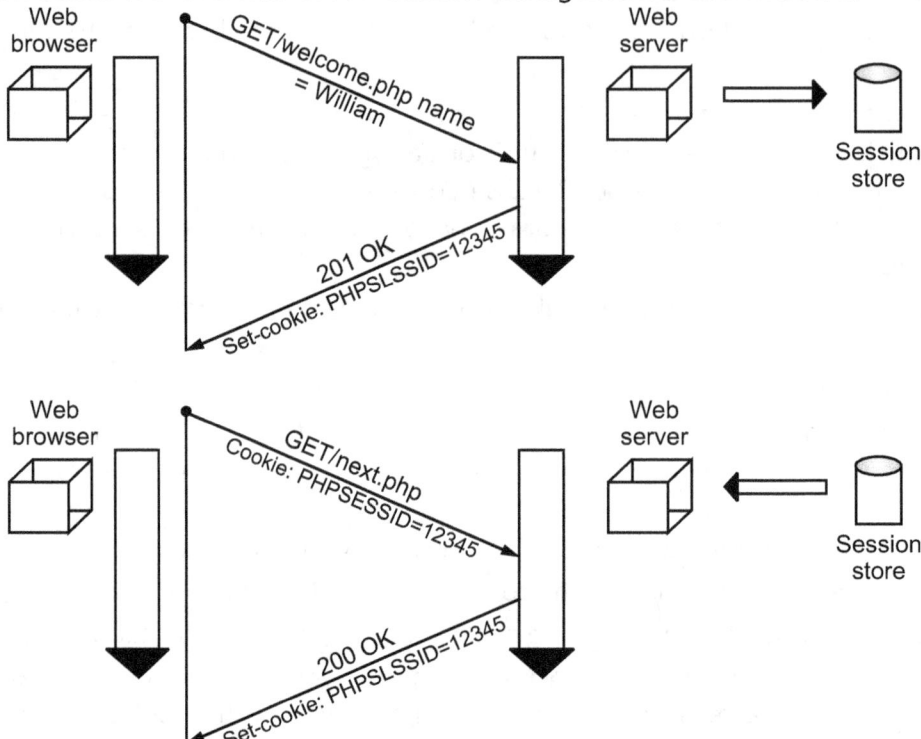

Fig. 2.3 : The interaction between the browser and the server when initial requests are made to session-based application

When user first enters the session-based application by making a request to a page that starts a session, PHP generates a session and creates a file that stores the session-related variables. PHP sets a cookie to hold the session ID in the response the script generates. The browser then records the cookie and includes it in subsequent requests. In the example shown above, the script welcome.php records session variables in the session store, and a request to next.php then has access to those variables because of the session ID.

The out-of-box configuration of PHP session management uses disk-based files to store session variables. Using files as the session store is adequate for most application in which the numbers of concurrent sessions are limited. A more scalable solution that uses a MySQL database as a session store.

Starting a Session :

PHP provides a session_start( ) function that creates a new session and subsequently identifies and establishes an existing one. Either way, a call to the session_start( ) function initializes a session.

The first time a PHP scripts calls session_start( ), a session identifier is generated and by default, a set-cookie header field is included in the response. The response sets up a session cookie in the browser with the name PHPSESSID and the value of the session identifier. The PHP session management automatically includes the cookie without the need to call to the setcookie( ) or header( ) functions.

The session identifier (ID) is a random string of 32 hexadecimal digits such as FCC17F261BCD8BF7F85CA281094390B4. As with other cookies, the value of the session ID is made available to PHP scripts in the $HTTP_COOKIE_VARS associative array and in the $PHPSESSID variable.

When a new session is started, PHP creates a session file. With the default configuration, session files are written in the /tmp directory using the session identifier, prefixed with sess_, for the filename. The filename associated with our example session ID is /tmp/sess_fcc17f261bcd8bf7f85ca281094300b4.

If a call is made to session_start( ) and the request contains the PHPSESSID cookie. PHP attempts to find the session file and initialize the associated session variables. However, if the identified session file can't be found, session_start( ) creates an empty session file.

You can unregister a variable from a session, which removes it from the data store, by calling session_unregister( ). The session_is_registered( ) function returns true if the given variable is registered. If you're curious, the session_id( )function returns the current session ID.

Example :

Simple PHP script that uses a session.

```
< ? PHP
// initialize a session. This call either creates a new session or
re-establishes an existing one.
    session_start ( );


// if this is a new session, then the variable $count will not be
registered
    if(! session_is_registered ("count"));
      {
        session_register ("count");
        session_register ("start");

        $count=0;
        $start=time ( );
      }
    else
```

```
{
    $cout ++;
}
    $session Id = session_id( );
? >
< ! doctype html public
    "-// w3c//DTD HTML 4.0 Transitional //EN"
    "http://www.w3.org/TR/html14/loose.dtd">
<html>
    <head> <title> sessions </title> </head>
    <body>
        <P> This page points at a session (<? = $session ID ?>)
        <br> count = <? = $count ?>
        <br> start = <? = $start ?>
        <P> This session has lasted
        <? php
            $duration = time( )-$start;
    echo "$duration";
        ?>
        seconds
        </body>
    </html>
```

Example :

Ending a session.: To end a session, call session_destroy( ). This removes the data store for the current session, but it doesn't remove the cookie from the browser cache. This means that, on subsequent visits to sessions-enabled pages, the user will have the same session ID she had before the call to session_destroy( ), but none of the data.

```
<? php
// Only attempt to end the session
// if there is a $phpsessid set by the request
if (isset ($PHPSESSID))
{
    $message = "<p> End of session ($ PHPSESSID)";
    session_start( );
    session_destroy( );
}
```

```
    else
    {
        $message = "<p> There was no session to destroy !";
    }
    ?>


    <! doctype html public
        "-// w3c//DTD HTML 4.0 Transitional //EN"
        "http://www.w3.org/TR/html4/loose.dtd">
    <html>
        <head> <title> sessions </title> </head>
        <body>
        <? = $message ?>
        </body>
    </html>
```

```
    <html>
    <head>
    <title>PHP example 1 </title>
    </head>
    <body>
    <h1> This is the first PHP example. </h1>
    <?
        printf("<h2> hello, world </h2>");
    ?>
    </body>
    </html>
```

To enable a session for a page, call session start( ) before any document being generated.

```
    <? php session_start ( ) ?>
    <html>
    ............
    ............
    </html>
```

This assigns a new session ID. The variable can be registered with the session by passing the name of the variable to the session_register( ) :

For example :

```
    <? php
```

```
session_start ( );
session_register ('no_of_hits');
++ $no_of_hits;
?>
```

The session_start( ) function loads registered variables into the associative array called $HTTP_SESSION_VARS. The variable will be unregistered which will be removed from the data store by calling session_unregistered( ). To end the session, call session_destroy( ). It will remove the data store for the current session, but will not remove the cookie from the browser cache.

For example :

```
<? php
    $c = array ('black' ⇒ '# 000000';
                'white' ⇒ '# ffffff');
session_start ( );
session_register ('bg');
$bg_name = $_POST['background'];
$bg = $c [$bg.now];
?>
```

Using preferences from sessions :

```
<? php
    session_start ( );
?>
    <html>
    <head> <title> hello </title> </head>
    <body bgcolour = "<?$bg ?>"
    <h1> hello world </h1>
    </body>
    </html>
```

Alternatives to Cookies

The session ID is passed from page to page which is stored in PHPSESSID cookie. PHP session supports two options form fields and URLs.

1. **Form field :** The session ID is passed via. hidden field. But here it forces you to make every link between pages to be forms submit button.
2. **URL :** Here the HTML files are rewritten by adding session ID to every relative link. But here the PHP must be configured with the enable_trans_id option, when complied. It is a lower process.

Custom Storage

By default, the session information is stored in files in server's temporary directory. Each session's variables are stored in the separate file. The location of the session files can be changed with session Save_path in PHP. ini file. The session information is stored in two formats.

1. PHP's built_in format.
2. WDDX (Web Distributed Data Exchange).

Here the session data in a database which will be shared between multiple sites. Here different functions are required for opening new session, closing a session, reading session information, writing session information, destroying a session etc.

To use the custom session store use the following code :

```
<Directory "/var/html/sample">
php_value session.save_handler user
php_value session.save.path mydb
php_value session.name session_store
</Directory>
```

Combining Cookies and Sessions

Using a combination of cookies and your own session handler, we can preserve state across visits. Sessions can handle which page the user is on. While cookie can store the states that persist between user visits, such as unique user ID. We will see simple example of this. Here user selects the text and the background colors and stores it in a cookie.

```
<? php
it ($_POST['bg color'])
{
 setcookie('bgcolor', &_POST ['bgcolor', time( ) + (60*60*24*7));
}
$bgcolor = empty ($bgcolor) ? 'White';
$bgcolor;
?>
<body bgcolor = "<? = $bgcolor ?>">
<form action = "<? = $PHP_SELF ?>" method = "POST">
                 <p> Background color;
<select name = "bgcolor">
<option value = "Blue" > Blue </option>
<option value = "Red" > Red </option>
<option value = "White"> White </option>
</select>
<input type = "submit">
</form>
</body>
```

2.7 SSL (Secure Socket Layer)

The Secure Sockets Layer (SSL) provides a secure channel over which regular HTTP requests and responses can flow. The encryption cannot control from PHP. So https://URL indicates a secure connection for the document.

The PHP page was generated in response to a request over an SSL connection, if the HTTP's entry in the $_SERVER array is set to 'on'. For preventing a page from being generated over a non-encrypted connection, use

```
if($_SERVER['HTTPS'] ! == 'on')
{
    die("Must be a secure connection");
}
```

Any form parameters entered by the user are sent a form over on insecure connection – a trivial packet sniffer can reveal them.

Practice Program

Q. Write a PHP script to create a login form with user name and password, once the user login, the second form should be display to accept the user details (roll_no, name, city). If the user does not enter information within specified time limit, expire his session and give the warning.

//login.html

Ans.
```
<html>
<head> <title> login form </title> </head>
<body>
<form method = 'POST' action = "login.php">
user name:
<input type = "text" name = "user">
password:
<input type = "password" size = "25">
<input type = "submit">
</form>
</body>
<html>
```

//login.php

```
<?php
$auth_yes = 0;
session_start ();
session_register ('t');
#tm = time ();
```

```
?>
<form method = "GET" action = "new.php">
Roll No:
<input type = "text" name = "rno">
name:
<input type = "text" name = "nm">
city:
<input type = "text" name = "ct">
<input type = "submit">
</form>
```

//new.php

```
<?php
  session_start()'
  $newt = $tm + 60;
  if($newt < time())
     echo "Time out";
  else
  {
     echo "Roll No = $_GET ['rno']";
     echo "Name = $_GET [nm']";
     echo "City = $_Get['ct']";
  }
  session_destroy();
?>
```

Practice Questions

1. What is HTTP ?
2. Explain Multivalued Parameters with examples.
3. Write a note on SSL (secure sockets layer).
4. How will you get information of uploaded file ?
5. What are Cookies and Sessions?
6. Explain different content types in Php.
7. What is the use of Multivalued Parameters in PHP?
8. Which are Web Variables used in PHP? Explain any 2 variables.
9. What is the use of session_start() function in PHP?
10. What is a sticky form ?

☚☚☚

Chapter 3...

Databases

Contents ...

3.1 Introduction

In this Chapter, you will learn how to fetch data from the database, how to store data in the database, how to handle errors. A database consists of one or more tables. With PHP, you can connect to and manipulate databases. MySQL is the most popular database system used with PHP.

PHP 5 and later can work with a MySQL database using:

• MySQLi extension (the "i" stands for improved)

• PDO (PHP Data Objects)

Earlier versions of PHP used the MySQL extension. However, this extension was deprecated in 2012.

PDO will work on 12 different database systems, where as MySQLi will only work with MySQL databases.

So, if you have to switch your project to use another database, PDO makes the process easy. You only have to change the connection string and a few queries. With MySQLi, you will need to rewrite the entire code - queries included.

Both are object-oriented, but MySQLi also offers a procedural API and support Prepared Statements.

3.2 Using PHP to Access a Database   [Oct. 2016]

There are two ways to access databases from PHP :

(a) Use a database - specific extension.

(b) Use the database - independent PEAR DB library.

In database specific extension, code is intimately tied to the database i.e. function names, parameters, error handling and so on are completely different in different database extensions. If we move from one database to other, it will involve significant changes to your code.

The PEAR DB, on the other hand, hides the database specific functions from you. Moving between database systems can be as simple as changing one line of your program. But here, features that are specific to a particular database are unavailable. Use of PEAR DB is little slower than use of database - specific extension.

PHP to Connect a MySQL Database

The most important step of integrating MYSQL into your PHP script is connecting to the database. And while it is not strictly necessary to close the connection, it is always good practice to tie up any loose ends. Here we will learn how to do both.

- The mysqli_connect() function is used to connect the database. It requires four parameters, in the following order: mysqli_connect(servername, username, password, databasename)
- The value of "servername" will specify what server you need to connect to. Since the database is usually on the same server as the script/connection, the default value is "localhost".
- The username and password should be self-explanatory. Your web host probably provided them already. The database name is whatever you named your database.

```php
<?php
//ENTER YOUR DATABASE CONNECTION INFO BELOW:
$hostname="localhost";
$database="mydb";
$username="username";
$password="myPassword";

//DO NOT EDIT BELOW THIS LINE
$link = mysqli_connect($hostname, $username, $password);
if (!$link) {
die('Connection failed: ' . mysql_error());
}
else{
    echo "Connection to MySQL server " .$hostname . " successfully
connected!" . PHP_EOL;
}
$db_selected = mysql_select_db($database, $link);
if (!$db_selected)
```

```
{
    die ('Can\'t select database: ' . mysql_error());
}
else {
    echo 'Database ' . $database . ' successfully selected!';
}

mysql_close($link);
mysqli_close($link);
?>
```

In above code, we have connected to our database and stored the connection details/handle in the $link variable for later reference. Then we tested our connection using the handle and told the script to stop working if the connection was faulty. And last but not least, we used mysqli_close() to close the open connection.

PHP Create MySQL Tables

The CREATE TABLE statement is used to create a table in MySQL.

We will create a table named "MyGuests", with five columns: "id", "firstname", "lastname", "email" and "reg_date":

```php
<?php
$servername = "localhost";
$username = "username";
$password = "password";
$dbname = "myDB";

// Create connection
$conn = mysqli_connect($servername, $username, $password, $dbname);
// Check connection
if (!$conn) {
    die("Connection failed: " . mysqli_connect_error());
}

// sql to create table
$sql = "CREATE TABLE MyGuests (
id INT(6) UNSIGNED AUTO_INCREMENT PRIMARY KEY,
firstname VARCHAR(30) NOT NULL,
lastname VARCHAR(30) NOT NULL,
```

```
email VARCHAR(50),
reg_date TIMESTAMP
)";

if (mysqli_query($conn, $sql))
{
    echo "Table MyGuests created successfully";
}
 else
{
    echo "Error creating table: " . mysqli_error($conn);
}

mysqli_close($conn);
?>
```

After the data type, you can specify other optional attributes for each column:

NOT NULL: Each row must contain a value for that column, null values are not allowed

DEFAULT value: Set a default value that is added when no other value is passed

UNSIGNED: Used for number types, limits the stored data to positive numbers and zero

AUTO INCREMENT: MySQL automatically increases the value of the field by 1 each time a new record is added

PRIMARY KEY: Used to uniquely identify the rows in a table. The column with PRIMARY KEY setting is often an ID number, and is often used with AUTO_INCREMENT.

Running MYSQL Queries In PHP

The mysql_query() function is a "catch all" that can run about any MYSQL query that you give it. Let's look into the execution of some standard insert, select, update and delete statements.

```
<?php
  $con = mysqli_connect("localhost","my_username","my_secret_password",
"database_name");
   if (!$con) { die('Could Not Connect: ' . mysql_error($con) .
mysql_errno($con))}
   $insert = mysqli_query($con, "INSERT INTO table_name (col1, col2)
VALUES('Value 1', 'Value 2');")}
if (!$insert) { die (mysql_error($con));}
  $select = mysqli_query($con, "SELECT * FROM table_name;");
   if (!$select) { die (mysql_error($con));}
```

```
    $update = mysqli_query($con, "UPDATE table_name SET col2 = 'Value'
WHERE col2 LIKE 'Value 2';");
    if (!$update) {die (mysql_error($con));}
    $delete = mysqli_query($con, "DELETE FROM table_name WHERE col2 LIKE
'Value';");
    if (!$delete) { die (mysql_error($con)); }
    mysqli_close($con);
?>
```

As you can see, each time mysqli_query() is used, it can be assigned a handle that we can later use to identify the results of the statement. Also, the function is (optionally) given the opportunity to print out an error message and die if errors occurred during execution of the statement.

Insert Data Into MySQL Using MySQLi and PDO

After a database and a table have been created, we can start adding data in them.

Here are some syntax rules to follow:

- The SQL query must be quoted in PHP
- String values inside the SQL query must be quoted
- Numeric values must not be quoted
- The word NULL must not be quoted

The INSERT INTO statement is used to add new records to a MySQL table:

INSERT INTO table_name (column1, column2, column3,...)

VALUES (value1, value2, value3,...)

Select Data From a MySQL Database

The SELECT statement is used to select data from one or more tables:

SELECT column_name(s) FROM table_name

or we can use the * character to select ALL columns from a table:

SELECT * FROM table_name

Delete Data From a MySQL Table

The DELETE statement is used to delete records from a table:

DELETE FROM table_name

WHERE some_column = some_value

Update Data In a MySQL Table

The UPDATE statement is used to update existing records in a table:

UPDATE table_name

SET column1=value, column2=value2,...

WHERE some_column=some_value

```php
<?php
$servername = "localhost";
$username = "username";
$password = "password";
$dbname = "myDB";

// Create connection
$conn = new mysqli($servername, $username, $password, $dbname);
// Check connection
if ($conn->connect_error) {
    die("Connection failed: " . $conn->connect_error);
}

$sql = "UPDATE MyGuests SET lastname='Doe' WHERE id=2";

if ($conn->query($sql) === TRUE) {
    echo "Record updated successfully";
} else {
    echo "Error updating record: " . $conn->error;
}

$conn->close();
?>
```

3.3 MYSQL Database Functions   [April 2016]

PHP's MYSQLI class has over 60 built-in functions to meet your MYSQL interfacing needs.But we only concentrate on the fourteen functions that are most suited to our needs:

Function	Description
mysqli_affected_rows()	Returns the number of affected rows in the previous MySQL operation
mysqli_close()	Closes a previously opened database connection
mysqli_connect()	Opens a new connection to the MySQL server
mysqli_errno()	Returns the last error code for the most recent function call
mysqli_error()	Returns the last error description for the most recent function call

... (Contd.)

Function	Description
mysqli_fetch_all()	Fetches all result rows as an associative array, a numeric array, or both
mysqli_fetch_array()	Fetches a result row as an associative, a numeric array, or both
mysqli_fetch_assoc()	Fetches a result row as an associative array
mysqli_fetch_row()	Fetches one row from a result-set and returns it as an enumerated array
mysqli_free_result()	Frees the memory associated with a result
mysqli_num_rows()	Returns the number of rows in a result set
mysqli_query()	Performs a query against the database
mysqli_real_escape_string()	Escapes special characters in a string for use in an SQL statement
mysqli_select_db()	Changes the default database for the connection

3.4 Relational Databases and SQL

A Relational Database Management System (RDBMS) is a server that manages data for user. The data is structured into tables. A table is a collection of related data entries and it consists of columns and rows.

Each table has a number of columns, each of which has name and type. A relational database is based on the relational model and uses a collection of tables to represent both data and the relationships among those data. It also includes a DML and DDL. Most commercial relational database systems empty the SQL language.

Tables are grouped together into databases. An RDBMS has its own user system, which controls access rights for databases. Each table has multiple columns, and each column has a unique name. Tables 3.1, 3.2 and 3.3 presents a sample relational database.

The first table, the customer table, shows, for example, that the customer identified by customer_id 192-83-7465 is named Johnson and lives at 12 Alma St. in Palo Alto. The second table, account table shows, for example, that account A-101 has a balance of ₹ 500 and A-201 has table a balance of ₹ 900.

The third table, the depositor table shows which accounts belong to which customers. For example, account number A-101 belongs to the customer whose customer_id is 192-83-7465, namely Johnson and customers 192-83-7465 (Johnson) and (019-28-3746 (Smith) share account number A-201 (they may share a business venture).

The relational model is an example of a record-based model. Record-based models are so named because the database is structured in fixed-format records of several types. Each table contains records of a particular type. Each record type defines a fixed number of fields, or attributes. The columns of the table correspond to the attributes of the record type.

It is not hard to see how tables may be stored in files. For instance, a special character (such as comma) may be used to delimit the different attributes of a record, and another special character (such as a new-line character) may be used to delimit records. The relational model hides such low-level implementation details from database developers and users.

(a) The CUSTOMER table :

Table 3.1

customer_id	customer_name	customer_street	customer_city
192-83-7465	Johnson	12 Alma St.	Palo Alto
677-89-9011	Hayes	3 Main St.	Harrison
182-73-6091	Turner	123 Putnam Ave.	Stanford
321-12-3123	Jones	100 Main St.	Harrison
336-66-9999	Lindsay	175 Park Ave.	Pittsfield
019-28-3746	Smith	72 North St.	Rye

(b) The ACCOUNT table :

Table 3.2

account_number	balance
A-101	500
A-215	700
A-102	400
A-305	350
A-201	900
A-217	750
A-222	700

(c) The DEPOSITOR table :

Table 3.3

customer_id	account_number
192-83-7465	A-101
192-83-7465	A-201
019-28-3746	A-215
677-89-9011	A-102
182-73-6091	A-305
321-12-3123	A-217
336-66-9999	A-222
019-28-3746	A-201

PHP communicates with relational databases using Structured Query Language (SQL).

SQL

IBM developed the original version of SQL, originally called Sequel, as part of the System R project in the early 1970s. The Sequel language has evolved since then, and its name has changed to SQL (Structured Query Language). Many products now support the SQL language. SQL has clearly established itself as the standard relational database language.

The SQL language has several parts :

- **Data-Definition Language (DDL) :** The SQL DDL provides commands for defining relation schemas, deleting relations, and modifying relation schemas.
- **Interactive Data-Manipulation Language (DML) :** The SQL DML includes a query language based on both the relational algebra and the tuple relational calculus. It includes also commands to insert tuples into, delete tuples from, and modify tuples in the database.
- **Integrity :** The SQL DDL includes commands for specifying integrity constraints that the data stored in the database must satisfy. Updates that violate integrity constraints are disallowed.
- **View definition :** The SQL DDL includes commands for defining views.
- **Transaction Control :** SQL includes commands for specifying the beginning and ending of transactions.
- **Embedded SQL and Dynamic SQL :** Embedded and dynamic SQL define how SQL statements can be embedded within general-purpose programming languages, such as C, C++, Java, PL/I, Cobol, Pascal and Fortran.
- **Authorization :** The SQL DDL includes commands for specifying access rights to relations and views.

The SQL standard supports a variety of built-in domain types, including :

- **char(n) :** A fixed-length character string with user-specified length n. The full form, character, can be used instead.
- **varchar(n) :** A variable-length character string with user-specified maximum length n. The full form, character varying, is equivalent.
- **int :** An integer (a finite subset of the integers that is machine dependent). The full form, integer, is equivalent.
- **smallint :** A small integer (a machine-dependent subset of the integer domain type).
- **numeric(p, d) :** A fixed-point number with user-specified precision. The number consists of p digits (plus a sign), and d of the p digits are to the right of the decimal point. Thus, numeric (3, 1) allows 44.5 to be stored exactly, but neither 444.5 or 0.32 can be stored exactly in a field of this type.
- **real, double precision :** Floating-point and double-precision floating-point numbers with machine-dependent precision.
- **float(n) :** A floating-point number, with precision of atleast n digits.

SQL syntax is divided into two parts :

(a) DDL (Data Definition Language).

(b) DML (Data Manipulation Language).

(a) The DDL is used to create and modify the database structure. SQL provides a rich DDL that allows one to define tables, integrity constraints, assertions, etc.

For instance, the following statement in the SQL language defines the account table :

```
create table account
    (account_number char(10),
    balance integer)
```

Execution of the above DDL statement creates the account table. In addition, it updates the data dictionary, which contains metadata. The schema of a table is an example of metadata.

(b) The DML is used to retrieve and modify data in an existing database. The query language of SQL is non-procedural. It takes as input several tables (possibly only one) and always returns a single table. Here is an example of an SQL query that finds the names of all customer who reside in Harrison :

```
select customer.customer_name
from customer
where customer.customer.city = 'Harrison'
```

The query specifies that those rows from the table customer where the customer_city is Harrison must be retrieved, and the customer_name attribute of these rows must be displayed. More specifically, the result of executing this query is a table with a single column labeled customer_name, and a set of rows, each of which contains the name of a customer whose customer_city is Harrison. If the query is run on the preceding Tables 1.1, 1.2 and 1.3, the result will consist of two rows, one with the name Hayes and the other with the name Jones.

Queries may involve information from more than one table. For instance, the following query finds the account numbers and corresponding balances of all accounts owned by the customer with customer_id 192-83-7465.

```
select account.account_number, account.balance
from depositor, account
where depositor.customer_id = '192-83-7465' and
depositor.account_number = account.account_number
```

If the above query was run on the preceding tables, the system would find that the two accounts numbered A-101 and A-201 are owned by customer 192-83-7465 and the result will consist of a table with two columns (account_number, balance) and two rows (A-101, 500) and (A-201, 900).

Basic Structure of SQL Query

A relational database consists of a collection of relations, each of which is assigned a unique name. SQL allows the use of null values to indicate that the value either is unknown or does not exist. It allows a user to specify which attributes cannot be assigned null values.

The basic structure of an SQL expression consists of three clauses : **select, from,** and **where**.

- The **select** clause corresponds to the projection operation of the relational algebra. It is used to list the attributes desired in the result of a query.

- The **from** clause corresponds to the Cartesian-product operation of the relational algebra. It lists the relations to be scanned in the evaluation of the expression.

- The **where** clause corresponds to the selection predicate of the relational algebra. It consists of a predicate involving attributes of the relations that appear in the from clause.

That the term select has different meaning in SQL than in the relational algebra is an unfortunate historical fact.

A typical SQL query has the form,

> **select** $A_1, A_2, ..., A_n$
>
> **from** $r_1, r_2, ..., r_m$
>
> **where** P

Each A_i represents an attribute and each r_i a relation. P is a predicate. The query is equivalent to the relational-algebra expression.

$$\Pi_{A_1, A_2, ..., A_n} (\sigma_P (r_1 \times r_2 \times ... \ r_m))$$

If the where clause is omitted, the predicate P is true. However, unlike the result of a relation-algebra expression, the result of the SQL query may contain multiple copies of some tuples.

SQL forms the Cartesian product of the relations named in the from clause, performs a relation-algebra selection using the where clause predicate, and then projects the result onto the attributes of the select clause. In practice, SQL may convert the expression into an equivalent form that can be processed more efficiently.

Some of The Most Important SQL Commands

```
SELECT - extracts data from a database.
```

Syntax :

```
SELECT column_name1,column_name2
FROM table_name;
```

Example :

```
SELECT * FROM Customers;
```

3.11

UPDATE Command : updates data in a database

Syntax :

```
UPDATE table_name
SET column1=value1,column2=value2,...
WHERE some_column=some_value;
UPDATE Customers
```

Example :

```
SET ContactName='Alfred Schmidt', City='Hamburg'
WHERE CustomerName='Alfreds Futterkiste';
```

DELETE Command : deletes data from a database

Syntax :

```
DELETE FROM table_name
WHERE some_column=some_value;
```

Example :

```
DELETE FROM Customers
WHERE CustomerName='Alfreds Futterkiste' AND ContactName='Maria
Anders';
```

INSERT INTO Command: inserts new data into a database

Syntax :

```
INSERT INTO table_name
VALUES (value1,value2,value3,...);
```

Example :

```
INSERT INTO Customers (CustomerName, ContactName, Address, City,
PostalCode, Country)
VALUES ('Cardinal','Tom B. Erichsen','Skagen
21','Stavanger','4006','Norway');
```

CREATE DATABASE Commands : creates a new database

Syntax :

```
CREATE DATABASE DatabaseName;
```

Example :

```
CREATE DATABASE testDB;
```

ALTER DATABASE Command : modifies a database

```
ALTER {DATABASE | SCHEMA} [db_name]
    alter_specification ...
```

CREATE TABLE Command : creates a new table

Syntax :

```
CREATE TABLE table_name(
column1 datatype,
column2 datatype,
column3 datatype,
.....
columnN datatype,
PRIMARY KEY( one or more columns )
);
```

Example :

```
SQL> CREATE TABLE CUSTOMERS(
ID    INT            NOT NULL,
NAME VARCHAR (20)    NOT NULL,
AGE  INT            NOT NULL,
ADDRESS  CHAR (25) ,
SALARY   DECIMAL (18, 2),
PRIMARY KEY (ID)
);
```

ALTER TABLE Command : modifies a table

Syntax :

```
ALTER TABLE table_name {ADD|DROP|MODIFY} column_name {data_ype};
```

DROP TABLE Command : deletes a table

Syntax :

```
DROP TABLE table_name;
```

CREATE INDEX Command : creates an index (search key)

Syntax :

```
CREATE INDEX index_name
ON table_name (column_name);
```

DROP INDEX Command : deletes an index

Syntax :

```
DROP INDEX index_name;
```

Index :

```
DROP INDEX ord_customer_ix_demo;
```

Assuming you have a table called customer, this SQL statement would insert a new row:

```
INSERT INTO customer VALUES(12, 'Raghvan', 2000, 2);
```

- This SQL statement inserts a new row but lists the columns for which there are values:

```
INSERT INTO customer (name, year, deptname) VALUES ('Shravan', 2013, 4);
```

- To delete all movies from 1980, we could use this SQL statement:

```
DELETE FROM customer WHERE year=1980;
```

- To change the year for Raghvan to 2000, use this SQL statement:

```
UPDATE customer SET year=2000 WHERE name='Raghvan';
```

- To select only customers that have salary more than 7000, use:

```
SELECT * FROM customer WHERE salary > 7000;
```

- You can also specify the fields you want returned. For example:

```
SELECT name, salary FROM customer WHERE salary >= 6000 AND salary < 12000;
```

You can issue queries that bring together information from multiple tables. For example, this query joins together the customer and department tables to let us see who is working in which department:

```
SELECT customer.name, customer.year, department.name
FROM customer,department WHERE customer.deptid = department.deptid;
```

3.5 Pear DB Basics   [Oct. 2016]

Here, we will see how to use the PEAR DB library to connect to a database, issue queries, check for errors and transform the results of queries into HTML. The library is object-oriented with a mixture of class methods.

```
[DB::Connect(), DB::isError()] and object methods [$db→query(),
$q → fetchInto ( )]
```

Example 3.1 :

```
<html>
    <head>
    <title> Library Books </title>
    </head>
    <body>
    <table>
    <tr>
        <th> Book </th>
        <th> Year published </th>
        <th> Author </th>
    </tr>
    <?php
```

```php
//connect
require_once ('DB.php');
$db = DB::Connect ("mysql://librarian:password @
        localhost/Library");
if (DB::isError ($db))
{
   die ($db -> getMessage ( ));
}
//issue the query
$sql = "SELECT books·title, book·pub_year,
      authors.name FROM books, authors
      WHERE books.authorid = authors.authorid
      ORDER BY books·pub_year ASC";
$q = $db -> query($sql);
if (DB::isError($q))
{
   die ($q -> getMessage( ));
}
//generate the table
while ($q -> fetchInto($row))
{
   ?> <tr>
      <td>
        <? = $row [0] ?> </td>
      <td>
        <? = $row [1] ?> </td>
      <td>
        <? = $row [2] ?> </td>
      </tr>
   <? php
}
?>
```

Data Source Names

A Data Source Name (DSN) is a string that specifies where the database is located, username and password to use when connecting to the database. The components of a DSN in PEAR are assembled into a URL - like string.

type://username : password @ protocol + hostspec/database

The only mandatory field is 'type', which specifies the PHP database backend to use.

Here, protocol is the communication protocol to use. Two common values are 'tcp' and 'Unix' corresponding to Internet and UNIX domain socket. Every database backend does not support every communication protocol.

In our program, we connected to the 'MYSQL' database 'library' with the username 'librarian' and password 'password'.

Connecting

Once you have DSN, create a connection to the database using the connect ( ) method.

//$db = DB :: Connect (DSN [, option]);

The 'option' value can be Boolean, indicating whether or not the connection is to be persistent, or an array of options settings.

Error Checking

PEAR DB method return DB-ERROR if an error occurs. We can check for this with :

DB :: isError ( )

This method returns true if an error occurred while working with the database object. If there was an error, the usual behaviour is to stop the program and display the error message reported by getMessage ( ) method.

Issuing a Query

The query ( ) method on a database object sends SQL to the database.

$result = $db –> query (sql);

A SQL returns DB-OK to indicate success. SQL that performs a query returns an object that we can use to access the results.

Fetching Results from a Query

PEAR DB provides two methods for fetching data from query result object.

1.   Returns an array corresponding to the next row.
2.   Stores the row array into a variable passed as a parameter.

The fetchRow ( ) method on a query result returns an array of the next row of results.

$row = $result –> fetchRow ([mode]);

This returns either an array of data, NULL if there is no more data,

OR DB-ERROR if an error occurred.

Example : while ($row = $Result –> fetchRow ( ))

```
{
    if (DB::isError ($row))
    {
        die ($row -> getMessage ( ));
    }
}
```

Storing the Row :

The fetchInto ( ) method gets the next row and stores it into the array variable passed as a parameter.

It returns NULL if there is no more data, or DB-ERROR if an error occurs.

Example : while ($A = $result –> fetchInto ($row))

```
    {
        if (DB::isError ($A))
        {
            die ($A -> getMessage ( ));
        }

            ⋮

    }
```

Inside a Row Array :

By default, returned arrays are indexed arrays, where the positions in the array correspond to the order of the columns in the returned result.

Example : Var-dump ($row);

```
array 3
    {
        [0]  ⟹  string (5)  "PHP"
        [1]  ⟹  string (4)  "2010"
        [2]  ⟹  string (12)  "Kevin"
    }
```

OR

```
    Var_dump ($row);
    object (stdclass) (3)
    {
        ["title"]  ⟹  string (5)  "PHP"
        ["pub_year"]  ⟹  string (4)  "2010"
        ["name"]  ⟹  string (12)  "Kevin"
    }
To access the data,
    echo  "[$row -> title} was published in
            {$row -> pub_year} and author is
            {$row -> name}";
```

Finishing the Result:

Free ( ) method returns the memory consumed by the result of a query to the operating system.

> $ result –> free ( );

Free ( ) method is automatically called on all queries when the PHP script ends.

Disconnecting

All database connections are disconnected when the PHP script ends. But if we want to disconnect it forcefully then use disconnect ( ) method.

3.6 Advanced Database Techniques

PEAR DB provides several shortcut functions and separate prepare/execute steps that can improve the performance of repeated queries.

Placeholders

Pass the query ( ) function SQL with '?' in place of specific values and add a second parameter consisting of the array of values to insert into the SQL.

$db –> query ('Insert into books (title, pub_year) values (?, ?)')

There are 3 characters that we can use as placeholder values in SQL query :

1. ?   → A string or number, which will be quoted if necessary.
2. | → A string or number, which will never be quoted.
3. &   → A filename, the contents of which will be included in the statement.

Prepare/Execute

When issuing the same query repeatedly, more efficient way is to compile the query once and then execute it multiple times using prepare ( ), execute ( ) and executeMultiple ( ) methods.

prepare ( ) is used to compile the query.

Example : $C = $db –> prepare (SQL);

execute ( ) fills in any placeholders in the query and sends to the RDBMS.

Example : $r = $db –> execute (c, values);

Here, the values array contains the values for the placeholders in the query. The returned value is either a query response object or DB_ERROR if an error occurred.

Example :

```
$A = array (array (1, 'Kapil'),
            array (2, 'Sunil'),
            array (3, 'Ravi'));
$C = $q -> prepare ('Insert into A (RN, Name) values (?,?)');
For each ($A as $B)
```

```
{
    $db -> execute ($C, $B);
}
```

The executeMultiple ( ) method takes a two dimensional array of values to insert.

```
$r = $db -> executeMultiple (c, values);
```

The compiled query i.e. 'c' is executed once for every entry in values and query responses are collected in $r.

Example :

```
$A = array (array (1, 'Kapil'),
             array (2, 'Sunil'),
             array (3, 'Ravi'));
$C = $q -> prepare ('Insert into A (RN, Name) values (?,?)');
$db -> insertMultiple ($C,$A);
```

Shortcuts

```
getOne ( ), getRow ( ), getCol ( ), getAssoc ( ), getAll ( )
methods permits placeholders.
```

getOne ( ): It fetches the first column of the first row of data returned by an SQL query.

```
Syntax :
    $V = $db -> getOne (SQL [, values]);
```

Example :

```
$x = $db -> getOne ("Select Name From A where RN = 5");
if (DB::isError ($x))
{
    die ($x -> getMessage ( ));
}
echo $x;
```

getRow ( ) : It returns the first row of data returned by an SQL query :

```
    $row = $db -> getRow (SQL [, values]);
```

If you want to return only one row, this method is useful.

Example : List ($RN, $Name) = $db -> getRow ("Select RN, Name From A where RN = 5");
echo "($RN, $Name)";

getCol ( ) : It returns a single column from the data returned by an SQL query.

```
    $C = $db -> getCol (SQL [, column (, values)]);
```

The 'column' parameter can be either a number or column name.

(0 is the default value and indicates first column).

getALL ( ) returns an array of all the rows returned by the query.

```
$all = $db -> getAll (SQL [, values [, fetchmode]]);
```

All the get * ( ) methods return DB_ERROR when an error occurs.

Details About a Query Response

The **numRows ( )** and **numCols ( )** methods tell you the number of rows and columns returned from a 'SELECT' query.

The **affectedRows ( )** method tells you the number of rows affected by an INSERT, DELETE or UPDATE operation.

The **tableInfo ( )** method returns detailed information on the type and flags of fields returned from a 'select' operation.

Sequences

PEAR DB sequences are an alternative to database - specific ID assignment.

The nextID ( ) returns the next ID for the given sequence.

```
$id = $db -> nextID (sequence);
```

A sequence is really a table in the database that keeps track of the last assigned ID. We can explicitly create and destroy sequences with the createSequence ( ) and dropSequence ( ) methods.

```
$r = $db -> createSequence (Sequence);

$r = $db -> dropSequence (Sequence);
```

The result will be DB_ERROR if error occurred.

Metadata

The getListOF ( ) method lets you query the database for information on available databases, users, views and functions.

```
$data = $db -> getListOF (A);
```

The parameter A is a string identifying the database features to list. Some databases support 'databases', 'users', 'views', 'functions'.

```
// $dbs = $db -> getListOF ("databases");
```

This example stores a list of available databases in $dbs.

Transactions

Some RDBMS support transactions, in which a series of database changes can be committed or rolled back. PEAR DB offers the commit ( ) and rollback ( ) methods to help with transactions.

```
$r = $db -> commit ( );

$r = $db -> rollback ( );
```

If we use databases that doesn't support transactions, then method returns DB_ERROR.

3.7 Sample Application   [Oct. 2016]

Two HTML forms are needed to populate the database tables. One form provides the site administrator with the means to add category IDs, titles, and descriptions. The second form, used by the self-registering businesses, collects the business contact information and permits the registrant to associate the listing with one or more categories. A separate page displays the listings by category on the web page.

There are three tables: businesses to collect the address data for each business, categories to name and describe each category, and an associative table called biz_categories to relate entries in the other two tables to each other. These tables and their relationships are shown in following Figure

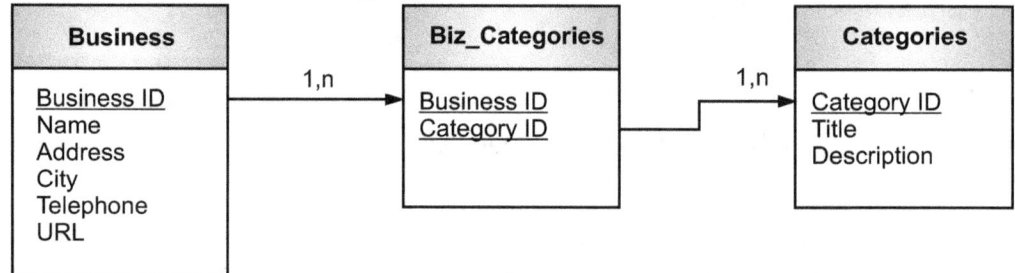

Fig. 3.1 : Database design for business listing service

```
Table structure for table 'biz_categories'

CREATE TABLE biz_categories (
    business_id int(11) NOT NULL,
    category_id char(10) NOT NULL,
    PRIMARY KEY (business_id, category_id),
    KEY business_id (business_id, category_id)
);

 Table structure for table 'business'

CREATE TABLE business (
    business_id int(11) NOT NULL auto_increment,
    name varchar(255) NOT NULL,
    address varchar(255) NOT NULL,
    city varchar(128) NOT NULL,
    telephone varchar(64) NOT NULL,
    url varchar(255),
    PRIMARY KEY (business_id),
```

```
   UNIQUE business_id (business_id),
   KEY business_id_2 (business_id)
);


 Table structure for table 'categories'

CREATE TABLE categories (
   category_id varchar(10) NOT NULL,
   title varchar(128) NOT NULL,
   description varchar(255) NOT NULL,
   PRIMARY KEY (category_id),
   UNIQUE category_id (category_id),
   KEY category_id_2 (category_id)
);
```

Database Connection :

```php
<?php
   require_once ('DB.php');
   $username = 'user';
   $password = 'seekrit';
   $hostspec = 'localhost';
   $database = 'phpbook';
   $phptype = 'mysql';
   $dsn = "$phptype://$username:$password@$hostspec/$database";
   $db = DB::connect ($dsn);
   if (DB::isError ($db))
   {
      die ($db → getMessage ( ));
   }
   ?>
```

Backend Administration Page : The backend page that allows administrators to add categories to the listing service. The input fields for adding a new record appear after a dump of the current data. The administrator fills in the form and presses the Add Category button, and the page redisplays with the new record. If any of the three fields are not filled in, the page displays an error message.

```
<html>
<head>
<?php
   require_once ('db_login.php');
?>
<title>
<?php
   $doc_title = 'Category Administration';
   echo "$doc_title \n";
?>
</title>
</head>
<body>
<h1>
<?php
$Cat_ID = $_REQUEST ['Cat_ID'];
$Cat_Title = $_REQUEST ['Cat_Title'];
$Cat_Desc = $_ REQUEST ['Cat_Desc'];
$add_record = $_REQUEST ['add_record'];
$len_Cat_id = strlen ($_REQUEST ['Cat_ID']);
$len_Cat_tl = strlen ($_REQUEST ['Cat_Title']);
$len_Cat_de = strlen ($_REQUEST ['Cat_Desc']);
if ($add_record = = 1)
{
   if ($len_Cat_id>0) and ($len_Cat_tl>0) and ($len_Cat_de>0))
   {
      $sql = "insert into categories (category_id, title,
              description)";

      $sql = "values ('$Cat_ID', '$Cat_title',
              '$Cat_Desc')";
      $result = $db -> query ($sql);
      $db -> commit( );
   }
}
```

```
$sql = "select * from categories";
$result = $db -> query ($sql);
?>
<Form method = "post" action = "<? = $PHP_SELF
   ?> ">
<table>
<tr> <th bgcolor = "eeeeee"> CatID </th>
   <th> Title </th>
   <th> Description </th>
</tr>
<?php
while ($row = $result -> fetchRow ( ))
{
   echo "<tr> <td> $row[0]</td> <td> $row[1] </td>
   <td> $row[2] </td> <?tr> \n";
}
?>
<tr> <td> <input type = "text" name = "Cat_ID"
            Size = "15" maxlength = "10"/> </td>
      <td> <input type = "text" name = "Cat_title"
            Size = "40" maxlength = "128" /> </td>
      <td> <input type = "text" name = "Cat_Desc"
            Size = "45" maxlength = "255" /> </td>
</tr>
</table>

<input type = "hidden" name = "add_record"
         value = "1" />
<input type = "Submit" name = "Submit"
         value = "Add Category" />
</body>
</html>
```

When the administrator submits a new category, we construct a query to add the category to the database. Another query displays the table of all current categories. Fig. 3.2 shows the page with five records loaded.

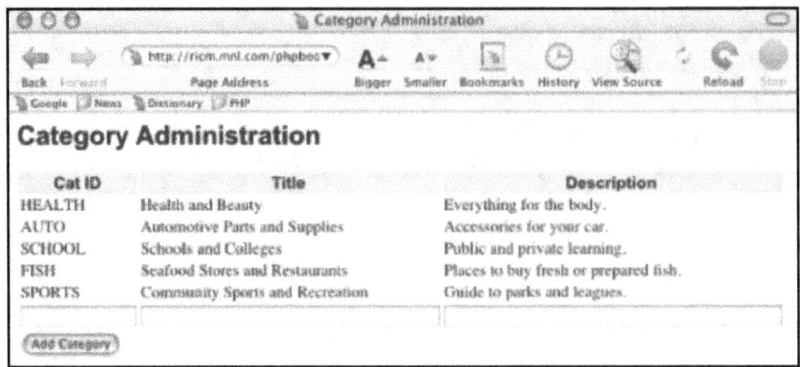

Fig. 3.2 : The administration page

Adding a Business :

This page lets a business insert data into the business and biz_categories tables. Fig. 3.3 shows the form.

Fig. 3.3 : The business registration page

When the user enters data and clicks on the Add Business button, the script calls itself to display a confirmation page. Fig. 3.4 shows a confirmation page for a company listing assigned to two categories.

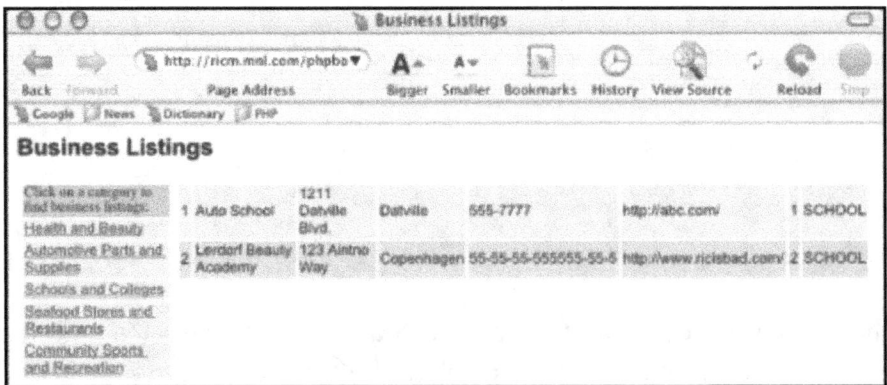

Fig. 3.4 : Confirmation page

```
<html>
<head>
<title>
<?php
   $doc_title = 'Business Registration';
   echo "$doc_title \n";
?>
</title>
</head>
<body>
<h1>
<? = $doc_title ?>
</h1>
<?php
   require_once ('db_login.php');
   $add_record = $_REQUEST ['add_record'];
   $Biz_Name = $_Request ['Biz_Name'];
   $Biz_Address = $_REQUEST ['Biz_Address'];
   $Biz_City = $_REQUEST ['Biz_City'];
   $Biz_Telephone = $_REQUEST ['Biz_Telephone'];
   $Biz_URL = $_REQUEST ['Biz_URL'];
   $Biz_Category = $_REQUEST ['Biz_Categories'];
   $Pick_Message = 'Click';
   %Pick_Message = 'Categories:';
   if ($add_record ==1)
   {
      $sql = 'Insert into business (name, address, city,
               telephone;
      $sql = url) values (?, ?, ?, ?, ?)';
      $params = array ($Biz_Name, $Biz_Address,
               $Biz_City, $Biz_Telephone, $Biz_URL);
      $query = $db -> prepare ($sql);
      if (DB::isError ($query)) die ($query -> getMessage ( ));
      $resp = $db -> execute ($query, $$params)
      if (DB::isError ($resp)) die ($resp -> getMessage ( ));
      $resp = $db -> commit ( );
```

```
            if (DB::isError ($resp)) die ($resp -> getMessage ( ));
            $biz_id = $db -> getOne ('Select max (business_ID)
                    From business);
        }
?>
<form method = "post" action = "<? = $PHP_SELF ?> ">
<table>
<tr> <td class = "picklist"> <? = $pick_message ?>
    <Select name = "Biz_Categories [ ]" Size = "4" multiple>
<?php
$sql = "SELECT" * FROM categories";
$result = $db -> query ($sql);
if (DB::isError ($result)) die ($result -> getMessage ( ));
while ($row = $result -> fetchRow ( ))
{
    if (DB::isError ($row)) die ($row → getMessage ( ));
    if ($add_record ==1)
    $selected = false;
    if (in_array ($row[1], $Biz_Categories))
    {
        $sql = 'Insert into Biz_categories;
        $sql = '(business_ID, category_id)
        $sql = 'values (?, ?)';
        $params = array ($biz_id, $row [0]);
        $query = $db -> prepare ($sql);
        if (DB::isError($query)) die($query -> getMessage ( ));
        $resp = $db -> execute ($query, $params);
        if(DB::isError ($resp)) die ($resp -> getMessage ( ));
        $resp = $db -> commit ( );
        if (DB:: isError ($resp)) die ($resp -> getMessage ( ));
        echo "$row[1]\n";
        $selected = true;
    }
    if ($selected == false)
```

```
    {
    echo "<option> $row[1] </option> \n";
    }
}
else
{
    echo "<option> $row[1] </option> \n";
}
?>
</select>
</td>
<td class = "picklist">
<table>
    <tr> <td class = "formlabel"> Business Name </td>
    <td> <input type = "text" name = "Biz_name"
        Size = "40" maxlength = "225"
        Value = "<? = $Biz_Name ?> "1> </td>
    </tr>
    <tr> <td> Address </td>
    <td> <input type = "text" name = "Biz_Address"
        Size = "40" maxlength = "225"
        Value = "<? = $Biz_Address ?>" /> </td>
    </tr>
    <tr> <td> City </td>
    <td> <input type = "text" name = "Biz_City"
        Size = "40" maxlength = "128"
        Value = "<? = $Biz_City ?>" /> </td>
    </tr>
    <tr> <td> Telephone </td>
    <td> <input type = "text" name = "Biz_Telephone"
        Size = "40" maxlength = "64"
        Value = <? = $Biz_Telephone ?>" /> </td>
    </tr>
    <tr> <td> URL </td>
    <td> <input type = "text" name = "Biz_URL"
        Size = "40" maxlength = "255"
```

```
            Value = "<? = $Biz_URL ?>" /> </td>
      </tr>
      </table>
      </td>
      </table>
      <input type = "hidden" name = "add_record"
         Value = "1" />
      <?php
   if ($add_record ==1)
   {
      echo '<a href ="  '$PHP_SELF'  "> Add another Bus </a>
   }
   else
   {
      echo '<input type = "submit" name = "submit"
         Value = "Add Business"/>';
   }
   ?>
   </body>
   </html>
```

Then last step is display the database.

Displaying the Database

Example shows a page that displays the information in the database. The links on the left side of the page are created from the categories table and link back to the script, adding a category ID. The category ID forms the basis for a query on the businesses table and the biz_categories table.

Example : Business listing page

```
<html>
<head>
<title>
<?php
 $doc_title = 'Business Listings';
 echo "$doc_title\n";
?>
```

```
</title>
</head>
<body>
<h1>
<?= $doc_title ?>
</h1>

<?php
 // establish the database connection

 require_once('db_login.php');

 $pick_message = 'Click on a category to find business listings:';
?>

<table>
<tr><td valign="top">
    <table>
    <tr><td class="picklist"><?= $pick_message ?></td></tr>
    <p>
    <?php
     // build the scrolling pick list for the categories
     $sql = "SELECT * FROM categories";
     $result = $db->query($sql);
     if (DB::isError($result)) die($result->getMessage( ));
     while ($row = $result->fetchRow( )){
         if (DB::isError($row)) die($row->getMessage( ));
         echo '<tr><td class="formlabel">';
         echo "<a href=\"$PHP_SELF?cat_id=$row[0]\">";
         echo "$row[1]</a></td></tr>\n";
     }
    ?>
    </table>
</td>
```

```php
<td valign="top">
    <table>
    <?php
     if ($cat_id) {
        $sql = "SELECT * FROM businesses b, biz_categories bc where";
        $sql .= " category_id = '$cat_id'";
        $sql .= " and b.business_id = bc.business_id";
        $result = $db->query($sql);
        if (DB::isError($result)) die($result->getMessage( ));
        while ($row = $result->fetchRow( )){
          if (DB::isError($row)) die($row->getMessage( ));
          if ($color == 1) {
            $bg_shade = 'dark';
            $color = 0;
          } else {
            $bg_shade = 'light';
            $color = 1;
          }
          echo "<tr>\n";
          for($i = 0; $i < count($row); $i++) {
            echo "<td class=\"$bg_shade\">$row[$i]</td>\n";
          }
          echo "</tr>\n";
        }
     }
    ?>
    </table>
</td></tr>
</table>
</body>
</html>
```

The business listings page is illustrated in Fig. 3.5.

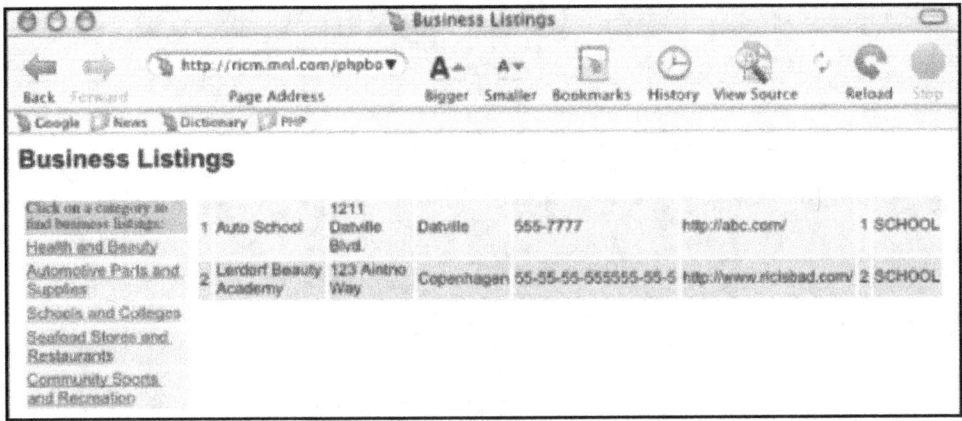

Fig. 3.5 : Business listings page

Practice Programs

Program - 1 :

PHP program to Update the Name of the student to 'xyz' whose roll no. is 1.

```php
<?php
$con=mysql_connect('localhost');
if (!$con)
    {
    die('Could not connect:' . mysql_error () );
    }
mysql_select_db("stud1", $con);
mysql_query("UPDATE stud2 SET name = 'xyz' where no. = 1");
$result = mysql_query('select * from stud2');
while($row = mysql_fetch_array($result))
    {
    echo "<td>" . $row['no'] . "</td>";
    echo "<td>" . $row['name'] . "</td>";
    }
mysql_close($con);
?>
```

Program - 2 :

PHP script to add and search the item from the database.

DBFirst.html

```
<form method='POST' action='First.php'>
<pre>
Item No : <input type='text' name='ino'>
Item Name :<input type='text' name='iname'>
Qty :
<input type='text' name='qty'>
<input type='radio' name='op' value='add'>
Add
   <input type='radio' name='op' value='search'>
Search
<input type='submit'>
<input type='reset'>
</pre>
</form>
```

First.php

```php
<?php
$con=mysql_connect("localhost", "root");
if (!$con)
   {
   die ('Could not connect:' . mysql_error());
   }
mysql_select_db("testDB", $con);
if($_POST['OP']=='add')
   {
   $ino=$_POST['ino'];
   $iname=$_POST['iname'];
   $qty=$_POST['qty'];
   $sql="Insert into item values ($ino, '$iname', $qty)";
mysql_query($sql);
   echo "Record inserted successfully";
elself($_POST ['OP']=='search')
   {
   $in = $_POST['iname'];
```

```
$result = mysql_query("Select item_no, item_name, qty from item
where item_name = '$in')";
while($row = mysql_fetch_array($result))
   {
   echo $row['item_no'];
   echo $row['item_name'];
   echo $row['qty'];
   }
mysql_close($con);
?>
```

Practice Questions

1. How do create database in MYsql?
2. Which are database functions of MYsql in PHP?
3. Which are built-in data types that SQL supports?
4. Which are types of languages used in SQL? Explain with example.
5. What is the difference between 'database specific extension' and 'database independent PEAR DB library' ?
6. What is Data Source Name in PEAR DB?
7. Explain the technique of 'Fetching' in PEAR DB.
8. What is meant by place holder ? Explain with example.
9. Explain prepare ( ) and execute ( ) method with example.
10. Explain sequences techniques in PHP?

✍ ✍ ✍

Chapter 4...

XML

Contents ...

4.1 Introduction to XML   [Oct. 2016]

XML stands for extensible Markup Language. As the name suggests, XML is a markup language like HTML. The XML specification was created by the World Wide Web Consortium (W3C), the body that sets standards for the web.

- XML and HTML were designed with different goals:
  1. XML was designed to transport and store data, with focus on what data is.
  2. HTML was designed to display data, with focus on how data looks.
- XML is self descriptive language it allows us to create our own tags to describe the data between them. We are not particularly interested in how the data will be presented and our main focus is ensuring that the data is well organized within descriptive tags or elements. This is because XML is primarily used for data storage and transfer purposes - not for presentation purposes.
- XML syntax refers to the rules that determine how an XML application can be written.
- The XML syntax is very straight forward, and this makes XML very easy to learn.

If we include an XML declaration, it must be the first item in our document. The XML declaration uses the <?xml?> element.

Example: `<?xml version="1.0" encoding="UTF-8" standalone="no"?>`

How can XML be used?

Use of XML :

XML is used in many aspects of web development, often to simplify data storage and sharing.

4.1

1. **XML separates data from HTML:**

    If we need to display dynamic data in our HTML document, it will take a lot of work to edit the HTML each time the data changes. With XML, data can be stored in separate XML files. This way we can concentrate on using HTML/CSS for display and layout, and be sure that changes in the underlying data will not require any changes to the HTML.

    With a few lines of JavaScript code, we can read an external XML file and update the data content of our web page.

2. **XML simplifies data sharing:**

    In the real world, computer systems and databases contain data in incompatible formats. XML stored data in plain text format. This provides a software- and hardware-independent way of storing data.

    This makes it much easier to create data that can be shared by different applications.

3. **XML simplifies data transport:**

    One of the most time-consuming challenges for developers is to exchange data between incompatible systems over the Internet.

    XML greatly reduces this complexity, since the data can be read by different incompatible applications.

4. **XML simplifies platform changes:**

    Upgrading to new systems i.e. hardware or software platforms, is always time consuming. Large amounts of data must be converted and incompatible data is often lost. XML stored data in text format. This makes it easier to expand or upgrade to new operating systems, new applications, or new browsers, without losing data.

5. **XML is used to create new internet languages:**

    A lot of new Internet languages are created with XML like XHTML, WSDL, WAP etc.

Features/Benefits of XML

XML has been widely adopted since its creation and with good reason. Some of the key features and benefits of XML include:

1. **Easy data exchange:** One of the great things about XML is that it can allow easy sharing of data between different applications - even if these applications are written in different languages and reside on different platforms.

2. **Self-describing data:** When we look at an XML document, it is very easy to figure out what's going on.

3. **Create our own languages:** XML allows us to specify our own markup language for our own specific purpose. Some existing XML based languages include Banking Industry Technology Secretariat (BITS), Bank Internet Payment System (BIPS) and so on.

Similar to an HTML document, XML documents consist of stuff at the top of the document, followed by the content. Consider the following XML example:

```
<?xml version="1.0" encoding="UTF-8" standalone="no"?>
<!DOCTYPE document system "xmltutorials.dtd">
<!-- Here is a comment -->
<?xml-stylesheet type="text/css" href="myStyles.css"?>
<xmltutorials>
  <tutorial>
    <name>XML Tutorial</name>
    <url>http://www.pragati.com/xml/tutorial</url>
  </tutorial>
  <tutorial>
    <name>HTML Tutorial</name>
    <url>http://www.pragati.com/html/tutorial</url>
  </tutorial>
</xmltutorials>
```

Following table provides an explanation of each part of the XML document in the above example.

Table 4.1 : XML Document

Prolog (optional)	XML Declaration	`<?xml version="1.0" encoding="UTF-8" standalone="no"?>`
	Document Type Definition (DTD)	`<!DOCTYPE document system "xmltutorials.dtd">`
	Comment	`<!-- Here is a comment -->`
	Processing Instructions	`<?xml-stylesheet type="text/css" href="myStyles.css"?>`
	White Space	
Elements and Content (required)	Root element opening tag	`<xmltutorials>`

	Child elements and content	`<tutorial>`
		  `<name>XML Tutorial</name>`
		`<url>http://www.pragati.com/xml/tutorial</url>`

| | | ```
</tutorial>
<tutorial>
   <name>HTML Tutorial</name>
   <url>http://www.pragati.com/html/tutorial</url>
</tutorial>
``` |
| | Root element closing tag | ```
</xmltutorials>
``` |

Here's a more detailed explanation of each part:

1. **Prolog:**

   Right at the top of the above Table 4.1, we have a prolog (also spelt prologue). A prolog is optional, but if it is included, it should become at the beginning of the document. The prolog can contain things such as the XML declaration, comments, processing instructions, white space and document type declarations. Although the prolog (and everything in it) is optional, it's recommended that we include the XML declaration in our XML documents.

   (i) XML Declaration: The XML declaration indicates that the document is written in XML and specifies which version of XML. The XML declaration, if included, must be on the first line of the document.

   The XML declaration can also specify the language encoding for the document (optional) and if the application refers to external entities (optional). In our example, we specify that the document uses UTF-8 encoding (although we do not really need to as UTF-8 is the default), and we specify that the document refers to external entities by using standalone="no". This is not a standalone document as it relies on an external resource i.e. the DTD.

   (ii) Document Type Definition (DTD): The DTD defines the rules of our XML document. Although XML itself has rules, the rules defined in a DTD are specific to our own needs. More specifically, the DTD allows us to specify the names of the elements that are allowed in the document, which elements are allowed to be nested inside other elements, and which elements can only contain data.

   The DTD is used when we validate our XML document. Any application that uses the document must stop processing if the document does not adhere to the DTD.

   DTDs can be internal i.e. specified within the document or external i.e. specified in an external file. In our example, the DTD is external.

   (iii) Comments: XML comments begin with <!-- and end with -->. Similar to HTML comments, XML comments allow us to write code within our document without it being parsed by the processor. We normally write comments as an explanatory note to ourself or another programmer. Comments can appear anywhere within our document.

<! ... This is a comment ...>

(iv) Processing Instructions: Processing instructions begin with `<?` and end with `?>`. Processing instructions are instructions for the XML processor. Processing instructions are not built into the XML recommendation. Rather, they are processor-dependant so not all processors understand all processing instructions. Our example is a common processing instruction that many processors understand. The instructions to the processor is to use an external style sheet.

(v) White Space: White space is simply blank space created by carriage returns, line feeds, tabs, and/or spaces. White space does not affect the processing of the document, so we can choose to include whitespace or not.

Technically, the XML recommendation specifies that XML documents use the UNIX convention for line endings. This means that we should use a linefeed character only (ASCII code 10) to indicate the end of a line.

There is a special attribute (`xml:whitespace`) that we can use to preserve whitespace within our elements.

2. Elements and Content:

This is where the document's content goes. It consists of one or more elements, nested within a single root element.

(i) Root Element Opening Tag: All XML documents must have one (and only one) root element. All other elements must be nested inside this root element. In other words, the root element must contain all other elements within the document. Therefore, the first tag in the document will always be the opening tag of the root element (the closing tag will always be at the bottom of the document).

(ii) Child Elements and Content: These are the elements that are contained within the root element. Elements are usually represented by an opening and closing tag. Data and other elements reside between the opening and closing tag of an element.

Although most elements contain an opening and closing tag, XML allows we to use empty elements. An empty element is one without a closing tag. We might be familiar with some empty elements used in HTML such as the <img> element or the <br> element. In XML, we must close empty elements with a forward slash before the > symbol. For example, <br />.

Elements can also contain one or more attributes. An attribute is a name/value pair, that we place within an opening tag, which allows us to provide extra information about an element. We may be familiar with attributes in HTML. For example, the HTML img tag requires the src attribute which specifies the location of an image (for example, `<img src="myImage.gif" />`).

(iii) Root Element Closing Tag: The last tag of the document will always be the closing tag of the root element. This is because all other elements are nested inside the root element.

XML Elements

An element of XML is everything from (including) the element's start tag to (including) the element's end tag.

An element can contain, other elements, text, attributes or a mix of all.

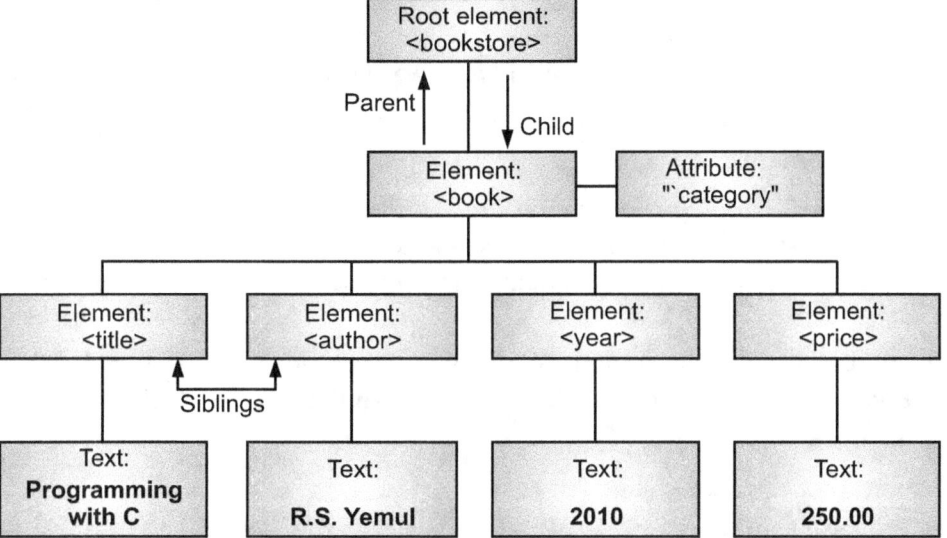

Fig 4.1: XML Tree

The image above represents one book in the XML below:

```
<bookstore>
  <book category="PROGRAMMING">
    <title>Programming with C</title>
    <author> R.S. Yemul</author>
    <year>2010</year>
    <price> ₹250.00</price>
  </book>
  <book category="WEB">
    <title>XML</title>
    <author>Umakant Shirshetti</author>
    <year>2012</year>
    <price> ₹180.00</price>
  </book>
</bookstore>
```

In the example above, <bookstore> and <book> have element contents, because they contain other elements. <book> also has an attribute (category="PROGRAMMING"). <title>, <author>, <year>, and <price> have text content because they contain text.

XML elements are represented by tags. Elements usually consist of an opening tag and a closing tag, but they can consist of just one tag.

Opening tags consist of <, followed by the element name, and ending with >. Closing tags are the same but have a forward slash inserted between the less than symbol and the element name.

Syntax: `<tag>contents............</tag>`

Empty elements are closed by inserting a forward slash before the greater than symbol.

`<tag/>`

Rules of XML Elements:

1. All elements must be closed properly:

In XML we must close all tags. This is usually done in the form of a closing tag where we repeat the opening tag, but place a forward slash before the element name (i.e. </child>).

If we are using an empty element i.e. one with no closing tag, we need to place a forward slash before the greater than symbol at the end of the tag (i.e. <child />).

Example for opening/closing tags:

`<child>Data............</child>` ...

2. Tags are case sensitive:

All tags must be written using the correct case. XML sees `<tutorial>` as a different tag to `<Tutorial>`.

Wrong: `<Tutorial>XML</tutorial>`

Right : `<Tutorial>XML</Tutorial>`

`<tutorial>XML</tutorial>`

`<TUTORIAL>XML</TUTORIAL>`

3. Elements must be nested properly:

We can place elements inside other elements but we need to ensure each element's closing tag does not overlap with any other tags.

Wrong: `<tutorial>`

`<name>XML</tutorial>`

`</name>`

Right : `<tutorial>`

`<name>XML</name>`

`</tutorial>`

4. Element Names:

We can use any name for elements, but follow the following rules:

(i)   Element names can contain any character including letters and numbers.

(ii) Element names must not contain spaces.

(iii) Element names must not begin with a number or punctuation character.

(iv) Element names must not start with the letters xml.

XML Attributes

XML elements can have attributes, just like HTML. Attributes provide additional information about an element.

We use attributes within our elements to provide more information about the element. These are represented as name/value pairs.

Syntax:

```
<tag attribute="value">Data or Contents here............</tag>
```

It is a most important to remember the following syntax rules when using attributes.

1. Quotes:

We must place quotation marks around the attribute's value.

Wrong:
```
<tutorials type=Web>
<tutorial>
    <name>XML and HTML</name>
</tutorial>
</tutorials>
```

Right :
```
<tutorials type="Web">
<tutorial>
    <name> XML and HTML</name>
</tutorial>
</tutorials>
```

2. Shorthand is prohibited:

Attributes must contain a value. Some HTML coders like to use shorthand, where if we provide the attribute name without a value, it will equal true. This is not allowed in XML.

Wrong:
```
<tutorials published>
<tutorial>
    <name>XML and HTML</name>
</tutorial>
</tutorials>
```

Right :
```
<tutorials published="true">
<tutorial>
```

```
       <name>XML and HTML</name>
   </tutorial>
   </tutorials>
```

Difference between HTML and XML

1. HTML was designed to display data with focus on how data looks while XML was designed to transport and store data, with focus on what data is.
2. HTML is a markup language itself while XML provides a framework for defining markup languages.
3. HTML is a presentation language while XML is neither a programming language nor a presentation language.
4. HTML is case insensitive while XML is case sensitive.
5. HTML is used for designing a web-page to be rendered on the client side while XML is used basically to transport data between the application and the database.
6. HTML has it own predefined tags while XML is flexible that custom tags can be defined and the tags are invented by the author of the XML document.
7. HTML is not strict if the user does not use the closing tags but XML makes it mandatory for the user the close each tag that has been used.
8. HTML does not preserve white space while XML does.
9. HTML is about displaying data, hence static but XML is about carrying information, hence dynamic.

4.2 XML Document Structure   [April 2016, Oct. 2016]

A typical XML structure looks much like an oddly named HTML file, although, for a number of reasons, most XML documents in use today are fairly highly structured. A simple example might be a purchase order which is shown below :

```
<?xml version= "1.0"?>
<purchaseOrder type = "1125" processed = "false">
<header>
   <orderFrom>Wiley E. Coyote</orderFrom>
   <orderTo>ACME Rocket Company </orderTo>
   <address>
      <street>1105 N. Sonoma Way</street>
      <city>Death Valley</city>
      <state>Arizona</state>
      </country>
   </address>
```

```
</header>
<body>
    <!-- The last rockets exploded prematurely. Please do watch
    your quality control. - WEC -->
    <lineItem>
        <name>Mark X Rocket</name>
        <description><![CDATA[Big, powerful red rockets, suitable
        for chasing highly mobile desert birds.]]></description>
            <number>24</number>
            <filter>if &gt; 15</filter>
            <unit>Individual</unit>
            <price>3.25</price>
            <priceUnit>USD</priceUnit>
            <discount>22.15</discount>
            <priceUnit>USD</priceUnit>
    </lineItem>
  </body>
</purchaseOrder>
```

While simple, this particular example shows most of the major elements of a stand-alone XML document (stand-alone in that there are no Document Type Definitions (DTDs) or schema information). In the preceding example, seven basic types of objects make up the document : processing instructions tags, elements tags, attributes, text, CDATA sections, entities, and comments.

1. Processing Instructions (PIs):

A processing instruction is bracketed by opening and closing question tags, as shown in the following example :

```
<? This is a processing instruction ?>
```

Processing instructions provide information outside of the normal scope of the XML structure for use by either the parser or third-party utilities. For example, you could use processing instructions to specify which display set to use when outputting the XML data. Formal XML structures should always start out with the <?xml version= "1.0"?> PI to indicate that this is an XML document, although most parsers will not generate errors if this first line is not included.

2. Elements :

An element consists of an open angle bracket immediately followed by a single word tag and zero or more name/value pairs (called attributes) terminated by a closing angle bracket, as shown in the following example :

```
<purchaseOrder type= "1125" processed= "false">
```

3. Attributes :

An attribute is a name/value pair that's associated with a given element. For example, in the purchaseOrder tag, both type and processed are the names of attributes, as shown in the following example :

```
<purchaseOrder type= "1125" processed= "false">
```

4. Comments :

A comment in an XML structure is a note added for clarification or coding purposes and is designated with an exclamation not and two dashes, as shown in the following example :

```
<!-- This is a single line note -->
```

Comments can include white space (such as character spaces, line breaks, tabs, and related elements) but can't include embedded comments. In other words,

```
<!-- This is a <!-- single --> line note -->
```

will generate an error since the close bracket after single is recognized only as the termination of the outermost comment.

5. Text :

Text in XML can be any Unicode character (that is, any 16-bit character encoding that follows the ISO Unicode standard), with a few important exceptions. While you can have XML tags embedded within text, XML treats these tags as subordinate elements Thus, while the following highlighted characters are considered to be text :

```
<name>Mark X Rocket</name>
```

only the words Mark and Rocket are considered to be text elements :

```
<name>Mark <X/Rocket</name>
```

6. CDATA Sections:

There are times when you want to include markup text in an XML document but you don't want the text to be parsed as part of the document. For example, you may have descriptive text that's marked up in HTML; you don't necessarily want this text to be interpreted as part of the XML document, especially if the HTML uses tags without terminators (such as the aforementioned <br> tag. This is the domain of CDATA sections, as shown in the following example :

```
<description><!CDATA]The <B>Mark X Rocket</B>
```

can be used for targeting highly mobile

```
<I>desert birds</I]]/description>
```

A CDATA (for character data) section is delimited by the somewhat unwieldy brackets, as in <![CDATA[and]]>. As with a comment, the only thing you can't put into a CDATA section is another CDATA section, since the closing brackets of]]> are the only way that the parser can tell where the CDATA section ends. CDATA sections retain information about line breaks and other white space, so they're actually quite useful for keeping things like JavaScript code in one piece.

7. Entities:

Entities come from SGML and let you use a convenient short names for longer blocks of text, even text that conceivably can contain additional XML markup (or even contain entire documents). XML currently supports only a handful of inbuilt entities, including &1t; (less than) for the <character, > (greater than) for >, and & (ampersand) to represent the & character. In the preceding XML structure, the filter element's text contains an entity, as shown in the following line :

```
<filter>if &gt; 15</filter>
```

When the text is later retrieved, the output will end up looking like the following line :

```
if > 15
```

You can define the additional entities through Document Type Definitions, and the current draft of the XML Schema specification calls for an equivalent structure called an XML variable.

There are two types of XML documents :

1. Well-formed
2. Valid.

A 'well-formed' XML document follows the basic syntax rules and a 'valid' document also follows the rules imposed by a DTD (Document Type Definition) or an XML schema.

Being well-formed is the most basic requirement for XML documents; one that is not well-formed is not really an XML documents. A well-formed XML document may contain any elements, attributes, or other constructs allowed by the XML specification.

A 'well-formed' document does not need to be 'valid', but a 'valid' document must be 'well-formed'. An XML document is valid if the elements, attributes and so on that it contains follow the rules in the DTD or schema. The purpose of having DTD or schema is to define exactly what elements and attributes are allowed and exactly what data they can contain.

Major Parts of an XML Documents

   (a) XML documents should contain an XML version line.
   (b) 'Valid' XML documents contain a DTD or an XML schema, or a reference to one of these if they are stored externally.
   (c) XML documents usually contain one or more elements, each of which may have one or more attributes. Elements can contain other elements or data.
   (d) XML documents may contain additional component such as processing instructions that provide machine instructions for particular applications.

Example of an XML document that is both well-formed and valid :

```
<?XML Version = "1.0" Standalone = "no"?>
<!DOCTYPE Client SYSTEM http://www.ex.com/dtds/Client.dtd"
<Clients>
    <Client> Joe </Client>
    <Client> Jim </Client>
<Clients>
```

Well-formed XML Documents

Syntax of well-formed XML follows some basic rules :

(a) Only one parent element in the document.

(b) Documents should begin with an XML declaration that gives in XML version number.

(c) If a document contains a DTD or a reference of XML schema that must appear before the first in the document.

(d) XML elements can be made from start and end tags or can be a single tag with a terminator.

(e) XML elements must be properly nested.

<parent> <child> ---- </child> </parent>

Using XML Elements and Attributes

There can be only one root element and it may contain multiple elements of the same name and child elements can also contain multiple elements of the same name.

```
<clients>
    <clients ID = "1"> Joe </client>
    <orders>
        <order ID = "1"> Product A </order>
        <order ID = "2"> Product B </order>
    </orders>
    <client ID = "2"> Jim </client>
    <orders>
        <order ID = "1"> Product A </order>
        <order ID = "2"> Product B </order>
    </orders>
<client>
    </clients>
```

Valid XML Documents : DTDs and XML Schemas

XML actually does have a second internal definition language called the Document Type Definitions (DTD), which is based on the older SGML DTD standards. While DTD implementations are more prevalent in the XML community, they suffer from a number of limitations compared to schemas.

DTDs are special documents which is not an XML language and therefore is not so easy to parse. XML schemas serve the same purpose, but are written in the XML schema language and can easily be parsed and processed using the same application that was used to read the XML document.

An XML Schema has essentially two types of actions: definition and declaration.

Definition : A node's characteristics are defined - the node's name, the data type, the type of enclosing content it can contain, and the order in which that content appears. Within an element's definition, there may very well be one or more child-element declarations.

Declaration : The declaration indicates how many times the given element can appear, within its parent and such a declaration, in turn, must have a definition for the given element further down the tree.

Specifically, XML schemas offer the following benefits over traditional DTDs:

- They are written in XML and can be referenced through a standard XML parser.
- They maintain data information about given node contents.
- They let you explicitly place limits on the number of elements contained within a structure, as well as whether a given XML node's contents is closed or open.
- They are tied into namespaces, letting you load multiple schemas into the same document. (DTD-based documents, on the other hand, must be declared through a command node, and a document can only have one DTD, although that DTD can provisionally include or exclude other DTDs.)
- You can define entities within XML Schemas using XML, making them easier to manipulate.
- You can define archetypes within an XML schema, giving you the bias for inheritance, encapsulation, and other OOP features.

Web Services

Web service is the name given to a unit of programmed logic that is available across the Internet, and the name XML web service is applied when the web service is accessible via XML languages for accessing such services.

Accessing predefined functions by simply identifying them by their URL and name and passing the appropriate parameters. It means you could build an application that is theoretically distributed anywhere across the Internet.

4.3 PHP and XML   [April 2016, Oct. 2016]

PHP (recursive acronym for PHP: Hypertext Preprocessor) is a widely-used open source general-purpose scripting language that is especially suited for web development and can be embedded into HTML.

PHP started out as a small open source project that evolved as more and more people found out how useful it was. Rasmus Lerdorf unleashed the first version of PHP way back in 1994.

- PHP is a server side scripting language that is embedded in HTML. It is used to manage dynamic content, databases, session tracking, even build entire e-commerce sites.
- It is integrated with a number of popular databases, including MySQL, PostgreSQL, Oracle, Sybase, Informix, and Microsoft SQL Server.
- PHP is pleasingly fast in its execution, especially when compiled as an Apache module on the Unix side. The MySQL server, once started, executes even very complex queries with huge result sets in record-setting time.
- PHP supports a large number of major protocols such as POP3, IMAP, and LDAP. PHP4 added support for Java and distributed object architectures (COM and CORBA), making n-tier development a possibility for the first time.

Five important characteristics make PHP's practical nature possible −Simplicity, Efficiency, Security, Flexibility, Familiarity.

There have been PHP functions available for connecting to, retrieving, manipulating data in databases. PHP has added functions that make it easier to work with XML documents.

Because of the nature and format of XML documents, much of the work on adding XML functions to PHP has centred on property parsing XML documents. To effectively parse and manipulate XML documents, these functions need to be able to get and work with the names and values of elements and attributes as well as many other components. PHP has added functions that make it easier to work with XML documents. These functions are as follows:

Here are a few of the most common functions :

- **xml_parser_create :** This is the basic function to create an xml parser, which can then be used with the other XML functions for reading and writing data, getting errors, and a variety of other useful tasks. Use xml_ parser_free to free up the resource when done.
- **xml_parse_into_struct :** Parse XML data into an array structure. You can use this function to take the contents of a well-formed XML file, turn it into a PHP array, and then work with the contents of the array.

- **xml_get_error_code :** Gets XML parser error code (defined as constants, such as XML_ERROR_NONE and XML_ERROR_SYNTAX). Use xml_error_string to get the textual description of the error based on the error code.

- **xml_set_option :** There are several options that can be set for an xml parser; XML_OPTION_CASE_FOLDING and XML_OPTION_TARGET_ENCODING. The case folding disabled. Target encoding enables you to specify which encoding is used for the target; the default is the encoding used by xml_parser_create, which in turn is ISO-8859-1. Use xml_parser_get_option to find out what options are currently set for an xml parser.

There are also a number of other XML parser functions as follows :

- **utf8_decode :** Converts a string with ISO-8859-1 characters encoded with UTF-8 to single-byte ISO-8859-1

- **utf8_encode :** Encodes an ISO-8859-1 string to UTF-8

- **xml_error_string :** Get XML parser error string

- **xml_get_current_byte_index :** Get current byte index for an XML parser

- **xml_get_current_column_number :** Get current column number for an XML parser

- **xml_get_current_line_number :** Get current line number for an XML parser

- **xml_parse :** Start parsing an XML document

- **xml_parser_create_ns :** Create an XML parser with namespace support

- **xml_parser_free :** Free an XML parser

- **xml_set_character_data_handler :** Set up character data handler

- **xml_set_default_handler :** Set up default handler

- **xml_set_element_handler :** Set up start and end element handlers

- **xml_set_end_namespace_decl_handler :** Set up end namespace declaration handler

- **xml_set_external_entity_ref_handler :** Set up external entity reference handler

- **xml_set_notation_decl_handler :** Set up notation declaration handler

- **xml_set_object :** Use XML Parser within an object

- **xml_set_processing_instruction_handler :** Set up processing instruction (PI) handler

- **xml_set_start_namespace_decl_handler :** Set up start namespace declaration handler

- **xml_set_unparsed_entity_decl_handler :** Set up unparsed entity declaration handler

PHP 5's new **SimpleXML** module makes parsing an XML document, well, simple. It turns an XML document into an object that provides structured access to the XML.

To create a SimpleXML object from an XML document stored in a string, pass the string to **simplexml_load_string( )**. It returns a SimpleXML object.

Example

Try out following example :

```
<html>
   <body>

      <?php
         $note=<<<XML

         <note>
            <to>Alia Sharma</to>
            <from> Tulip </from>
            <heading>Project submission</heading>
            <body>Please check clearly </body>
         </note>

         XML;
         $xml=simplexml_load_string($note);
         print_r($xml);
      ?>


   </body>
</html>
```

It will produce the following result :

SimpleXMLElement Object ([to] => Alia Sharma [from] => Tulip [heading] => Project submission [body] => Please check clearly)

Note : You can use function **simplexml_load_file(filename)** if you have XML content in a file.

Generating an XML Document

SimpleXML is good for parsing existing XML documents, but you can't use it to create a new one from scratch.

The easiest way to generate an XML document is to build a PHP array whose structure mirrors that of the XML document and then to iterate through the array, printing each element with appropriate formatting.

Example

Try out following example :

```php
<?php
    $channel = array('title' => "What's For Dinner",
        'link' => 'http://menu.example.com/',
        'description' => 'Choose what to eat today.');

    print "<channel>\n";

    foreach ($channel as $element => $content) {
        print " <$element>";
        print htmlentities($content);
        print "</$element>\n";
    }

    print "</channel>";
?>
```

It will produce the following result –

```
<channel>
    <title>What's For Dinner</title>
    <link>http://menu.example.com/</link>
    <description>Choose what to eat today.</description>
</channel>
```

Some of the applications that arise because of PHP and XML combination are as follows:

- **Data processing :** PHP's XML functions make it possible to parse XML data and carry out commands based on the type of data encountered. With some clever coding, this can be used to easily convert XML-encoded data into browser compliant HTML output. You also can use PHP's XML functions to create a database from an XML document, or vice versa.

- **Data transformation :** PHP's XSLT extension brings the full power of XSLT processing to the language, making it possible to apply XSLT stylesheets to XML data. With support for a wide range of XSLT processing instructions, transforming data from one format to another becomes very simple.

- **Platform-independent information exchange :** PHP's WDDX functions make it possible to easily transfer information (including typed data like arrays) from one system to another using platform-neutral data structures. This capability is particularly useful for content publishers who need to disburse information to requesting clients on a periodic basis, yet have no control over the platform and operating environment of those clients. For example, news syndication services or stock market tickers. Because WDDX structures are platform-neutral, the PHP/ WDDX combination encourages interoperability by making it possible to exchange data between programming languages in a simple and elegant manner.

- **Remote process execution :** Support for XML-RPC implies that PHP scripts can trigger processes on remote servers by sending them messages encoded in XML. This makes it possible to access different web services directly from your PHP script using standard client-server protocols and create new types of web applications based on these services. These processes/scripts might be written in other languages such as Java, Python, Perl, and so on.

4.4 XML Parser   **[April 2016, Oct. 2016]**

All today's modern browsers have a built-in XML parser. An XML parser converts an XML document into an XML DOM object - which can then be manipulated with JavaScript.

An XML parser is designed to read XML and create a way for programs to use XML.

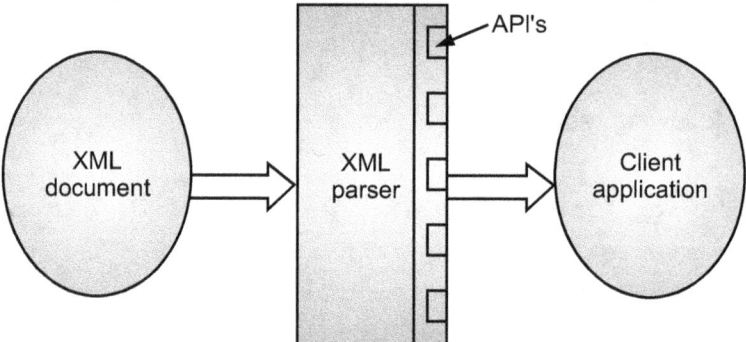

Fig 4.2 : XML Parser

To read and update - create and manipulate - an XML document, you will need an XML parser.

There are two basic types of XML parsers:

- **Tree-based parser:** This parser transforms an XML document into a tree structure. It analyzes the whole document, and provides access to the tree elements. e.g. the Document Object Model (DOM)

- **Event-based parser:** Views an XML document as a series of events. When a specific event occurs, it calls a function to handle it. E.g. Expat parser.

1. Parse an XML document:

The following program fragment parses an XML document into an XML DOM object.

```
if (window.XMLHttpRequest)
    {// code for IE7+, Firefox, Chrome, Opera, Safari
```

```
xmlhttp=new XMLHttpRequest();
}
else
{// code for IE6, IE5
xmlhttp=new ActiveXObject("Microsoft.XMLHTTP");
}
xmlhttp.open("GET","books.xml",false);
xmlhttp.send();
xmlDoc=xmlhttp.responseXML;
```

2. Parse an XML String:

The following program fragment parses an XML string into an XML DOM object.

```
txt="<bookstore><book>";
txt=txt+"<title>Web Technologies</title>";
txt=txt+"<author>Amar and Akbar</author>";
txt=txt+"<year>2013</year>";
txt=txt+"</book></bookstore>";

if (window.DOMParser)
  {
  parser=new DOMParser();
  xmlDoc=parser.parseFromString(txt,"text/xml");
  }
else // Internet Explorer
  {
  xmlDoc=new ActiveXObject("Microsoft.XMLDOM");
  xmlDoc.async=false;
  xmlDoc.loadXML(txt);
  }
```

3. XML file:

```
<?xml version="1.0" encoding="ISO-8859-1"?>
<html xsl:version="1.0"
xmlns:xsl="http://www.w3.org/1999/XSL/Transform"
xmlns="http://www.w3.org/1999/xhtml">
  <body style="font-family:Arial;font-size:12pt;background
                                           color:#EEEEEE">
    <xsl:for-each select="breakfast_menu/food">
```

```
      <div style="background-color:teal;color:white;padding:4px">
        <span style="font-weight:bold"><xsl:value-of
                                     select="name"/></span>
        - <xsl:value-of select="price"/>
      </div>
      <div style="margin-left:20px;margin-bottom:1em;font-size:10pt">
        <xsl:value-of select="description"/>
        <span style="font-style:italic">
          <xsl:value-of select="calories"/> (calories per serving)
        </span>
      </div>
    </xsl:for-each>
  </body>
</html>
```

Example:

```
<?xml version="1.0" encoding="ISO-8859-1"?>
<breakfast_menu>
    <food>
        <name>Meduwada</name>
        <price> 35.00</price>
        <description>two Meduwadas in a dish</description>
        <calories>420</calories>
    </food>
    <food>
        <name>Uttapa</name>
        <price> 40.00</price>
        <description>light for breakfast, made of onion, tomato etc.
</description>
        <calories>450</calories>
    </food>
    <food>
        <name>Toast</name>
        <price> 25.00</price>
        <description>Thick slices made from our homemade sourdough
bread</description>
        <calories>300</calories>
```

```
</food>
<food>
   <name>Homestyle Breakfast</name>
   <price> 60.00</price>
   <description>Two eggs and toast</description>
   <calories>800</calories>
</food>
</breakfast_menu>
```

4. XML DOM Parser

- Number of browsers have a built-in XML parser to read and manipulate XML.
- The parser converts XML into a JavaScript accessible object i.e. the XML DOM.
- The XML DOM contains methods or functions to traverse XML trees, access, insert, and delete nodes.
- However, before an XML document can be accessed and manipulated, it must be loaded into an XML DOM object.
- An XML parser reads XML, and converts it into an XML DOM object that can be accessed with JavaScript.
- Most browsers have a built-in XML parser. The DOM interfaces creates a tree structure based on the XML document.
- DOM parser useful for applications that include changes or modifications (for example, adding or deleting elements etc.)

Example:

```
<!DOCTYPE html>
<body>
<script>
if (window.XMLHttpRequest)
  {
  xhttp=new XMLHttpRequest();
  }
else // for IE 5/6
  {
  xhttp=new ActiveXObject("Microsoft.XMLHTTP");
  }
xhttp.open("GET","books.xml",false);
xhttp.send();
xmlDoc=xhttp.responseXML;
```

```
document.write("XML document loaded into an XML DOM Object.");
</script>
</body>
</html>
```

The following code loads and parses an XML string:

```
<!DOCTYPE html>
<body>
<script>
text="<bookstore><book>";
text=text+"<title>Web Technologies</title>";
text=text+"<author>Umakant Shirshetti</author>";
text=text+"<year>2013</year>";
text=text+"</book></bookstore>";
if (window.DOMParser)
  {
  parser=new DOMParser();
  xmlDoc=parser.parseFromString(text,"text/xml");
  }
else // Internet Explorer
  {
  xmlDoc=new ActiveXObject("Microsoft.XMLDOM");
  xmlDoc.async=false;
  xmlDoc.loadXML(text);
  }
document.write("XML string is loaded into an XML DOM Object");
</script>
</body>
</html>
```

5. SAX Parser

- A parser that implements SAX i.e., a SAX Parser functions as a stream parser, with an event-driven API.
- The user defines a number of callback methods that will be called when events occur during parsing.
- SAX parser useful for applications like search and retrieval that do not change the XML tree.
- SAX stands for simple API for XML and its important characteristics is that as it reads each unit of XML, it creates an event that the calling program can use.

- The SAX interfaces creates a series of linear events based on the XML document.
- The SAX events include (among others):
  - XML Text nodes
  - XML Element Starts and Ends
  - XML Processing Instructions
  - XML Comments
- Some events correspond to XML objects that are easily returned all at once, such as comments. However, XML elements can contain many other XML objects, and so SAX represents them as does XML itself: by one event at the beginning, and another at the end. Properly speaking, the SAX interface does not deal in elements, but in events that largely correspond to tags.
- SAX parsing is unidirectional; previously parsed data cannot be re-read without starting the parsing operation again.
- There are many SAX-like implementations in existence. In practice, details vary, but the overall model is the same. For example, XML attributes are typically provided as extreme name and value arguments passed to element events, but can also be provided as separate events, or via a hash or similar collection of all the attributes.
- For another, some implementations provide "Init" and "Fin" callbacks for the very start and end of parsing; others don't. The exact names for given event types also vary slightly between implementations.

Example:

```
<?xml version="1.0" encoding="UTF-8"?>
 <DocumentElement param="value">
     <FirstElement>
         &#xb6; Some Text
     </FirstElement>
     <?some_pi some_attr="some_value"?>
     <SecondElement param2="something">
         Pre-Text <Inline>Inlined text</Inline> Post-text.
     </SecondElement>
 </DocumentElement>
```

- Above XML document, when passed through a SAX parser, will generate a sequence of events like the following:
  - XML Element start, named DocumentElement, with an attribute param equal to "value".
  - XML Element start, named FirstElement.

- o XML Text node, with data equal to "¶ Some Text" (note: certain white spaces can be changed).
- o XML Element end, named FirstElement.
- o Processing Instruction event, with the target some_pi and data some_attr="some_value" (the content after the target is just text; however, it is very common to imitate the syntax of XML attributes, as in this example).
- o XML Element start, named SecondElement, with an attribute param2 equal to "something".
- o XML Text node, with data equal to "Pre-Text".
- o XML Element start, named Inline.
- o XML Text node, with data equal to "Inlined text".
- o XML Element end, named Inline.
- o XML Text node, with data equal to "Post-text."
- o XML Element end, named SecondElement.
- o XML Element end, named DocumentElement.

- Note that the first line of the sample above is the XML Declaration and not a processing instruction; as such it will not be reported as a processing instruction event (although some SAX implementations provide a separate event just for the XML declaration).
- The result above may vary: the SAX specification deliberately states that a given section of text may be reported as multiple sequential text events. Many parsers, for example, return separate text events for numeric character references.
- Thus in the example above, a SAX parser may generate a different series of events, part of which might include:
- o XML Element start, named FirstElement.
- o XML Text node, with data equal to "¶" (the Unicode character U+00b6).
- o XML Text node, with data equal to " Some Text".
- o XML Element end, named FirstElement.

6. XML Expat Parser :

The Expat parser is an event-based parser.

Look at the following XML fraction:

```
<from>Jani</from>
```

An event-based parser reports the XML above as a series of three events:

- Start element: from
- Start CDATA section, value: Jani
- Close element: from

The XML Expat Parser functions are part of the PHP core. There is no installation needed to use these functions.

The XML file below will be used in our example:

```
<?xml version="1.0" encoding="ISO-8859-1"?>
<note>
<to>Tove</to>
<from>Jani</from>
<heading>Reminder</heading>
<body>Don't forget me this weekend!</body>
</note>
```

We want to initialize the XML parser in PHP, define some handlers for different XML events, and then parse the XML file.

Initializing the XML Parser Example

```php
<?php
//Initialize the XML parser
$parser=xml_parser_create();


//Function to use at the start of an element
function start($parser,$element_name,$element_attrs)
  {
  switch($element_name)
    {
    case "NOTE":
    echo "-- Note --<br />";
    break;
    case "TO":
    echo "To: ";
    break;
    case "FROM":
    echo "From: ";
    break;
    case "HEADING":
    echo "Heading: ";
    break;
    case "BODY":
    echo "Message: ";
    }
  }
```

```php
//Function to use at the end of an element
function stop($parser,$element_name)
   {
   echo "<br />";
   }

//Function to use when finding character data
function char($parser,$data)
   {
   echo $data;
   }

//Specify element handler
xml_set_element_handler($parser,"start","stop");

//Specify data handler
xml_set_character_data_handler($parser,"char");

//Open XML file
$fp=fopen("test.xml","r");

//Read data
while ($data=fread($fp,4096))
   {
   xml_parse($parser,$data,feof($fp)) or
   die (sprintf("XML Error: %s at line %d",
   xml_error_string(xml_get_error_code($parser)),
   xml_get_current_line_number($parser)));
   }

//Free the XML parser
xml_parser_free($parser);
?>
```

The output of the code above will be:

```
-- Note --
To: Tove
From: Jani
Heading: Reminder
Message: Don't forget me this weekend!
```

How it works:

- Initialize the XML parser with the xml_parser_create() function.
- Create functions to use with the different event handlers.
- Add the xml_set_element_handler() function to specify which function will be executed when the parser encounters the opening and closing tags.
- Add the xml_set_character_data_handler() function to specify which function will execute when the parser encounters character data.
- Parse the file "test.xml" with the xml_parse() function.
- In case of an error, add xml_error_string() function to convert an XML error to a textual description.
- Call the xml_parser_free() function to release the memory allocated with the xml_parser_create() function.

4.5 The Document Object Model (DOM)

The Document Object Model (DOM) is an application programming interface (API) for HTML and XML documents. It defines the logical structure of documents and the way a document is accessed and manipulated.

DOM defines the objects, properties and methods (interface) to access all XML elements. The DOM is separated into 3 different parts / levels:

- **Core DOM :** Standard model for any structured document
- **XML DOM :** Standard model for XML documents
- **HTML DOM :** Standard model for HTML documents

As XML DOM also provides an API that allows a developer to add, edit, move or remove nodes at any point on the tree in order to create an application.

Below is the diagram for the DOM structure which depicts that parser evaluates an XML document as a DOM structure by traversing through each nodes.

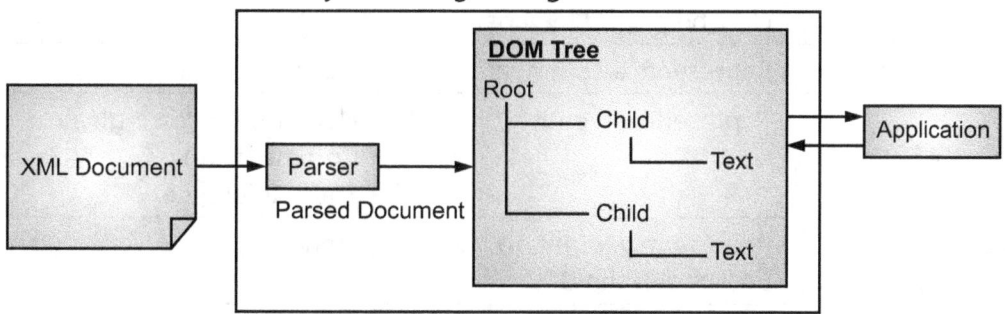

Fig 4.3 : DOM Structure

Let's see what a DOM structure is. A DOM document is a collection of nodes or pieces of information, organized in a hierarchy. Some types of nodes may have child nodes of various types and others are leaf nodes that cannot have anything below them in the document structure. Below is a list of the node types, and which node types they may have as children:

Table 4.2

Node Type	Description	Children
Document	Represents the entire document (the root-node of the DOM tree)	Element (max. one), ProcessingInstruction, Comment, DocumentType
Document fragment	Represents a "lightweight" document object, which can hold a portion of a document	Element, ProcessingInstruction, Comment, Text, CDATASection, EntityReference
DocumentType	Provides an interface to the entities defined for the document	None
ProcessingInstruction	Represents a processing instruction	None
EntityReference	Represents an entity reference	Element, ProcessingInstruction, Comment, Text, CDATASection, EntityReference
Element	Represents an element	Element, Text, Comment, ProcessingInstruction, CDATASection, EntityReference
Attr	Represents an attribute	Text, EntityReference
Text	Represents textual content in an element or attribute	None
CDATASection	Represents a CDATA section in a document (text that will NOT be parsed by a parser)	None
Comment	Represents a comment	None
Entity	Represents an entity	Element, ProcessingInstruction, Comment, Text, CDATASection, EntityReference
Notation	Represents a notation declared in the DTD	None

Example

Consider the DOM representation of the following XML document node.xml.

```
<?xml version="1.0"?>
<Company>
    <Employee category="technical">
```

```
    <FirstName>Tanmay</FirstName>
    <LastName>Patil</LastName>
    <ContactNo>1234567890</ContactNo>
</Employee>
<Employee category="non-technical">
    <FirstName>Taniya</FirstName>
    <LastName>Mishra</LastName>
    <ContactNo>1234667898</ContactNo>
</Employee>
</Company>
```

The Document Object Model of the above XML document would be as follows:

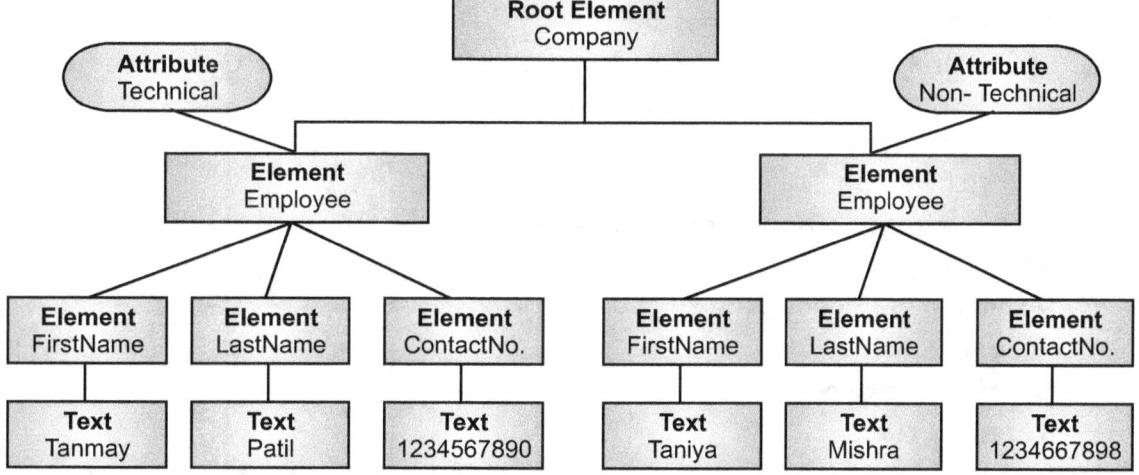

Fig 4.4 : Document Object Model of XML document

From the above diagram we can interface:

- Node object can have only one parent node object. This occupies the position above all the nodes. Here it is Company.

- The parent node can have multiple nodes called as child nodes. These child nodes can have additional node called as attribute node. In the above example we have two attribute nodes Technical and Non-Technical. The attribute node is not actually a child of the element node, but is still associated with it.

- These child nodes in turn can have multiple child nodes. The text within the nodes is called as text node.

- The node objects at the same level are called as siblings.

- The DOM Identifies:
  - the objects to represent the interface and manipulate the document.
  - the relationship among the objects and interfaces.

Nodes:

Every XML DOM contains the information in hierarchical units called Nodes and the DOM describes these nodes and the relationship between them.

The most common types of nodes in XML are:

- **Document Node:** Complete XML document structure is a document node.
- **Element Node:** Every XML element is an element node. This is also the only type of node that can have attributes.
- **Attribute Node:** Each attribute is considered as an attribute node. They contain information about an element node, but are not actually considered to be children of the element.
- **Text Node:** The document texts are considered as text node. It can consist of more information or just white space.

Some less common types of nodes are:

- **CData Node:** This node contains information that should not be analyzed by the parser. Instead, it should just be passed on as plain text.
- **Comment Node:** This node includes information about the data, and are usually ignored by the application.
- **Processing Instructions Node:** This node contains information specifically aimed at the application.
- **Document Fragments Node**
- **Entities Node**
- **Entity reference nodes**
- **Notations Node**

Node Tree :

In XML document the information is maintained in hierarchical structure, this hierarchical structure is referred as Node Tree. This hierarchy allows a developer to navigate around the tree looking for specific information, thus nodes are allowed to access. The content of these nodes can then be updated.

The structure of the node tree begins with the root element and spreads out to the child elements till the lowest level.

Example

Following example demonstrate simple XML document whose node tree is structure is shown in the diagram below:

```
<?xml version="1.0"?>
<Company>
    <Employee category="Technical">
        <FirstName>Tanmay</FirstName>
```

```
    <LastName>Patil</LastName>
    <ContactNo>1234567890</ContactNo>
</Employee>
<Employee category="Non-Technical">
    <FirstName>Taniya</FirstName>
    <LastName>Mishra</LastName>
    <ContactNo>1234667898</ContactNo>
</Employee>
</Company>
```

As can be seen in the above example whose pictorial representation (of its DOM) is as shown below:

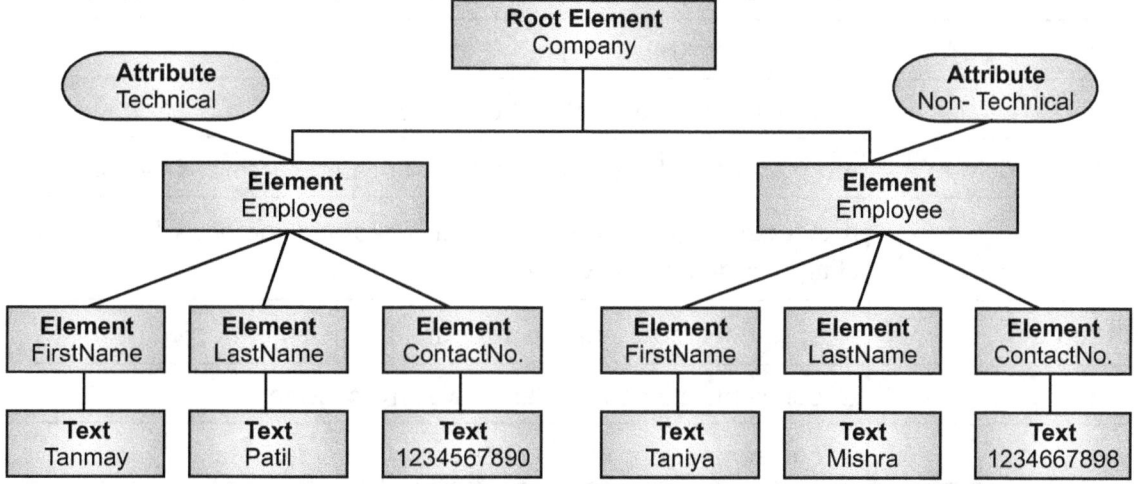

Fig. 4.5 : Pictorial representation of DOM example

- The topmost node of a tree is called the root. The root node is <Company> which in turn contains the two nodes of <Employee>. These nodes are referred to as child nodes.

- The child node <Employee> of root node <Company>, in turn consists of its own child node (<FirstName>, <LastName>, <ContactNo>).

- The two child nodes, <Employee> have attribute values Technical and Non-Technical, are referred as attribute nodes.

- The text within the every node is called as text node.

DOM as an API contains interfaces that represent different types of information that can be found in an XML document, such as elements and text. These interfaces include the methods and properties necessary to work with these objects. Properties define the characteristic of the node whereas methods give the way to manipulate the nodes.

Following table lists the DOM classes and interfaces:

Table 4.3

Interface	Description
DOMImplementation	It provides a number of methods for performing operations that are independent of any particular instance of the document object model.
DocumentFragment	It is is the "lightweight" or "minimal" document object, and it (as the superclass of Document) anchors the XML/HTML tree in a full-fledged document.
Document	It represents the XML document's top-level node, which provides access to all the nodes in the document, including the root element.
Node	It represents XML node.
NodeList	It represents a read-only list of Node objects.
NamedNodeMap	It represents collections of nodes that can be accessed by name.
Data	It extends Node with a set of attributes and methods for accessing character data in the DOM.
Attribute	It represents represents an attribute in an Element object.
Element	It represents element node. Derives from Node.
Text	It represents text node. Derives from CharacterData.
Comment	It represents comment node. Derives from CharacterData.
ProcessingInstruction	represents a "processing instruction". It is used in XML as a way to keep processor-specific information in the text of the document.
CDATA Section	Represents CDATA Section. Derives from Text.
Entity	It represents an entity. Derives from Node.
EntityReference	This represent an entity reference in the tree. Derives from Node.

Advantages
- XML DOM is language and platform independent.
- XML DOM is **travesible** - Information in XML DOM is organized in a hierarchy which allows developer to navigate around the hierarchy looking for specific information.
- XML DOM is **modifiable** - It is dynamic in nature providing developer a scope to add, edit, move or remove nodes at any point on the tree.

Disadvantages
- It consumes more memory (if the XML structure is large) as program written once remains in memory all the time until and unless removed explicitly.
- Due to the larger usage of memory its operational speed, compared to SAX is slower.

4.6 The Simple XML Extension

When it comes to sharing data, XML is the prevalent way to format information into a structure that is easily parsed. Your PHP application will need to parse XML at some point if you get data from APIs, including the API Twitter provides. Before Php 5, you had to build your own parser, looking in the string for patterns to divide up the formatted data in a meaningful way. Now, however, PHP comes with an extension called SimpleXML that does the heavy lifting for you.

The SimpleXML extension turns XML structures into embedded objects containing the data as associative arrays. Each embedded tag in the XML becomes another link in the PHP object, as in $xml->childnode->node['attribute']. The sample applications use SimpleXML to parse the data received from the Twitter API and to create new XML documents with the data the applications collect. The SimpleXML extension requires PHP 5.

Here are the methods you'll see :

1. SimpleXMLElement(well_formed_xml)

When you want to start building XML from scratch, SimpleXMLElement can help. It turns a well-formed XML string or a path to a file containing XML data into an object that can be iterated, edited, and expanded with a variety of methods. The object is a collection of tag names associated with the content the tags contain and the attributes they are assigned. Nested tags show up as objects that themselves can be parsed into tag names, attributes, and values.

```
$xml = new SimpleXMLElement($base_xml);
```

2. Simplexml_load_string(well_formed_xml_string)

For simply parsing XML data that already exists, this function takes the data in the form of a string and returns a navigable object.

```
$xml = simplexml_load_string($data);
```

3. getName ( )

The getName( ) method returns the name of the root tag for a particular XML object. When the XML object is first created, this will be the main root of the document, but this method can be used for nested objects as well.

```
$root = $xml->getName( );
```

4. children( )

The children( ) method creates an iterative array of objects representing the nodes directly below the XML object calling it. Each child object can then be explored for a name, value, attributes, or any other XML objects it contains.

```
foreach($xml->children( ) as $x) {$ids[] = $x->id;}
```

5. **addChild(name_of_new_node, value_stored_in_new_node)**

This method is what allows you to create your own XML documents. It accepts a text value to describe the name of the new nested tag and any value you want it to contain. It returns the new XML object, which can then be edited and expanded as if it had been part of the original XML.

6. **asXML( ):**

All of the manipulation of addChild( ) only changes the XML object that PHP has stored in memory. To make the changes real, you need to turn the object back into a string of well-formed XML text. This can be printed or stored in a string for later use in the application, as XML( ) will also accept a filename parameter and write the file directly to a document.

```
echo $xml->asXML( );
```

Example of SimpleXML

Get the node values from the **"note.xml"** file:

```
<note>
<to>Rajni</to>
<from>Jay</from>
<heading>Aditi</heading>
<body>Don't forget me this month!</body>
</note>
```

```
SimpleXML - Get Node Values
<!DOCTYPE html>
<html>
<body>

<?php
$xml=simplexml_load_file("note.xml")   or   die("Error:   Cannot
create object");
echo $xml->hello . "<br>";
echo $xml->How. "<br>";
echo $xml->are. "<br>";
echo $xml->you;
?>
</body>
</html>
```

Access an element's attributes with PHP's SimpleXML extension

The PHP SimpleXML extension makes it easy to work with XML files by creating an object from the XML structure. To access an element's attributes, use the property() method for that element.

The following examples use this as the XML string:

```
<data>
    <items>
        <item>
            <sometag myattribute="foo">A node</sometag>
        </item>
        <item>
            <sometag myattribute="bar">B node</sometag>
        </item>
    </items>
</data>
```

Get the "myattribute" attributes

First create the SimpleXML attribute. The above XML has already been loaded into a variable called $xml:

$xmlobj = new SimpleXMLElement($xml);

To access the value for the first <sometag> node from the first <item> do this:

echo $xmlobj->items->item[0]->sometag;

To access the "myattribute" attribute from the <sometag> node from the first <item> do this:

echo $xmlobj->items->item[0]->sometag->attributes()->myattribute;

To loop through all the <item> nodes and echo out the "myattribute" attribute and value for each of the <sometag> nodes do something along the lines of this:

```
foreach ($xmlobj->items->item as $item) {
  echo "Attribute: ". $item->sometag->attributes()->myattribute. "\n
      echo "Value: ". $item->sometag. "\n\n";
  }
```

This will output:

Attribute: foo

Value: A node

Attribute: bar

Value: B node

4.7 Changing a Value with Simple XML

The nodeValue property can be used to change the value of a text node.

books.xml :

```
<bookstore>
<book category="cooking">
<title lang="en">Everyday Italian</title>
```

```
<author>Giada De Laurentiis</author>
<year>2005</year>
<price>30.00</price>
</book>
<book category="children">
<title lang="en">Harry Potter</title>
<author>J K. Rowling</author>
<year>2005</year>
<price>29.99</price>
</book>
<book category="web">
<title lang="en">XQuery Kick Start</title>
<author>James McGovern</author>
<author>Per Bothner</author>
<author>Kurt Cagle</author>
<author>James Linn</author>
<author>Vaidyanathan Nagarajan</author>
<year>2003</year>
<price>49.99</price>
</book>
<book category="web" cover="paperback">
<title lang="en">Learning XML</title>
<author>Erik T. Ray</author>
<year>2003</year>
<price>39.95</price>
</book>
</bookstore>
```

The following code changes the text node value of the first <title> element:

```
<!DOCTYPE html>
<html>
<body>
<script>
if (window.XMLHttpRequest)
  {// code for IE7+, Firefox, Chrome, Opera, Safari
  xmlhttp=new XMLHttpRequest();
  }
else
```

```
{// code for IE6, IE5
xmlhttp=new ActiveXObject("Microsoft.XMLHTTP");
}
xmlhttp.open("GET","books.xml",false);
xmlhttp.send();
xmlDoc=xmlhttp.responseXML;

x=xmlDoc.getElementsByTagName("title")[0].childNodes[0];
x.nodeValue="Learn XML";
x=xmlDoc.getElementsByTagName("title")[0].childNodes[0];
txt=x.nodeValue;
document.write(txt);
</script>
</body>
</html>
```

Example Explained :

1. Load "books.xml" into xmlDoc using loadXMLDoc()
2. Get the text node of the first <title> element
3. Change the node value of the text node to "Learn XML"

Practice Questions

1. What is XML ?
2. Explain the source of XML document.
3. Write note on XML parser with example.
4. Explain few PHP DOM extension functions.
5. Explain few simpleXml extension functions.
6. Give an example of Changing the node value with simple XML.
7. Explain the terms:
    (a) XML Elements
    (b) XML Attributes
8. Write a note on DOM.

☝ ☝ ☝

Chapter 5...

Web Services

Contents ...

5.1 Web Services Concepts   [Oct. 2016]

Different books and different organizations provide different definitions to web services. Some of them are listed here.

   •   A web service is any piece of software that makes itself available over the internet and uses a standardized XML messaging system. XML is used to encode all communications to a web service. For example, a client invokes a web service by sending an XML message, then waits for a corresponding XML response. As all communication is in XML, web services are not tied to any one operating system or programming language--Java can talk with Perl; Windows applications can talk with Unix applications.

   •   Web services are self-contained, modular, distributed, dynamic applications that can be described, published, located, or invoked over the network to create products, processes, and supply chains. These applications can be local, distributed, or web-based. Web services are built on top of open standards such as TCP/IP, HTTP, Java, HTML, and XML.

   •   Web services are XML-based information exchange systems that use the Internet for direct application-to-application interaction. These systems can include programs, objects, messages, or documents.

   •   A web service is a collection of open protocols and standards used for exchanging data between applications or systems. Software applications written in various programming languages and running on various platforms can use web services to exchange data over computer networks like the Internet in a manner similar to inter-process communication on a single computer. This interoperability (e.g., between Java and Python, or Windows and Linux applications) is due to the use of open standards.

The basic web services platform is XML + HTTP. All the standard web services work using the following components

- SOAP (Simple Object Access Protocol)
- UDDI (Universal Description, Discovery and Integration)
- WSDL (Web Services Description Language)

Web Service Architecture

Web Service Roles:

There are three major roles within the web service architecture:

Service Provider : This is the provider of the web service. The service provider implements the service and makes it available on the Internet.

Service Requestor : This is any consumer of the web service. The requestor utilizes an existing web service by opening a network connection and sending an XML request.

Service Registry : This is a logically centralized directory of services. The registry provides a central place where developers can publish new services or find existing ones. It therefore serves as a centralized clearing house for companies and their services.

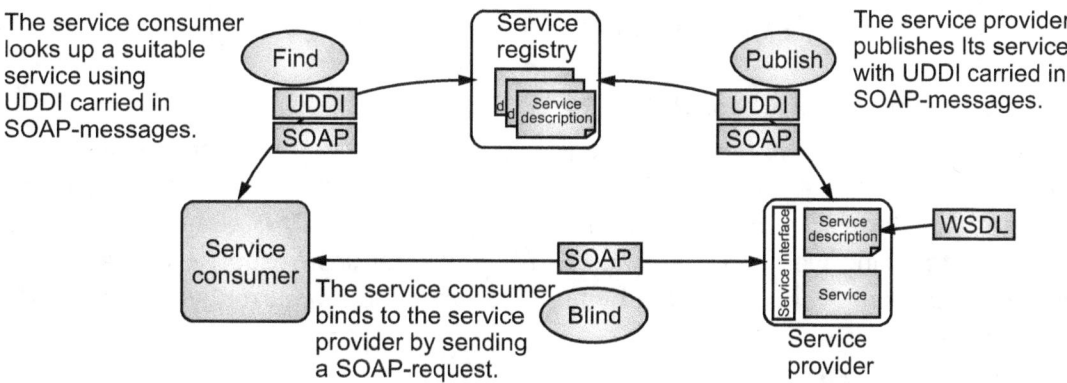

Fig 5.1: Components of Web Service Architecture

Web Service Protocol Stack

The architecture of a Web Services Stack varies from one organization to another. Fig. 5.1 illustrates the stack of specific, complementary standards on which web services are generally based on.

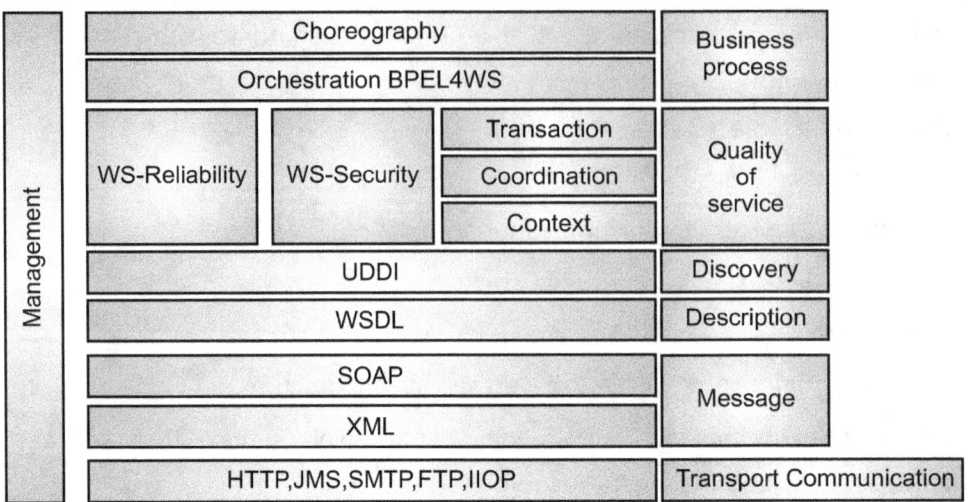

Fig. 5.2 : The Web Services Technology Stack

- **Service Transport**

  The service transport layer delivers messages between applications. This layer usually implements Hypertext Transfer Protocol (HTTP), Simple Mail Transfer Protocol (SMTP) , File Transfer Protocol (FTP) and newer protocols, such as Blocks Extensible Exchange Protocol (BEEP).

- **XML Messaging**

  This layer is responsible for encoding messages in a common XML format so that messages can be understood at either end. Currently, this layer includes XML-RPC and SOAP.

- **Simple Object Access Protocol (SOAP)**

  SOAP is a simple XML-based messaging protocol responsible for transferring data between different web services. It is built using XML and relies on common Internet transport protocol like HTTP to transport its messages. SOAP allows communication among interacting web services by implementing a request/response model and using HTTP to access networks protected by firewalls, which do not currently prevent HTTP and FTP service requests.

- **Service Description (WSDL)**

  The purpose of this layer is to define the public interface of a specific web service. Currently, service description is realized through the Web Service Description Language (WSDL) which is based on XML.

- **Service Discovery (UDDI)**

  The service discovery layer registers services into a common repository and provides an easy publish/find mechanism. This layer is often implemented via Universal Description, Discovery, and Integration (UDDI). But, the problem of service discovery is much discussed and the UDDI standard seems not to be used in large scale deployments.

- **Service Orchestration**

  The topmost service orchestration layer is in charge of the execution logic of web services based applications by determining their control flows (e.g. conditional, sequential, parallel and exceptional execution). This layer enables enterprises to define and realise complex business processes.

  With the ongoing evolution of web services, it is possible that more layers will be added to these different layers, for example Specifying Quality Of Services (QoS) aspects, may be added to the technology stack described above as well

How Does a Web Service Work?

A web service enables communication among various applications by using open standards such as HTML, XML, WSDL, and SOAP. A web service takes the help of:

- XML to tag the data
- SOAP to transfer a message
- WSDL to describe the availability of service.

You can build a Java-based web service on Solaris that is accessible from your Visual Basic program that runs on Windows.

You can also use C# to build new web services on Windows that can be invoked from your web application that is based on Java Server Pages (JSP) and runs on Linux.

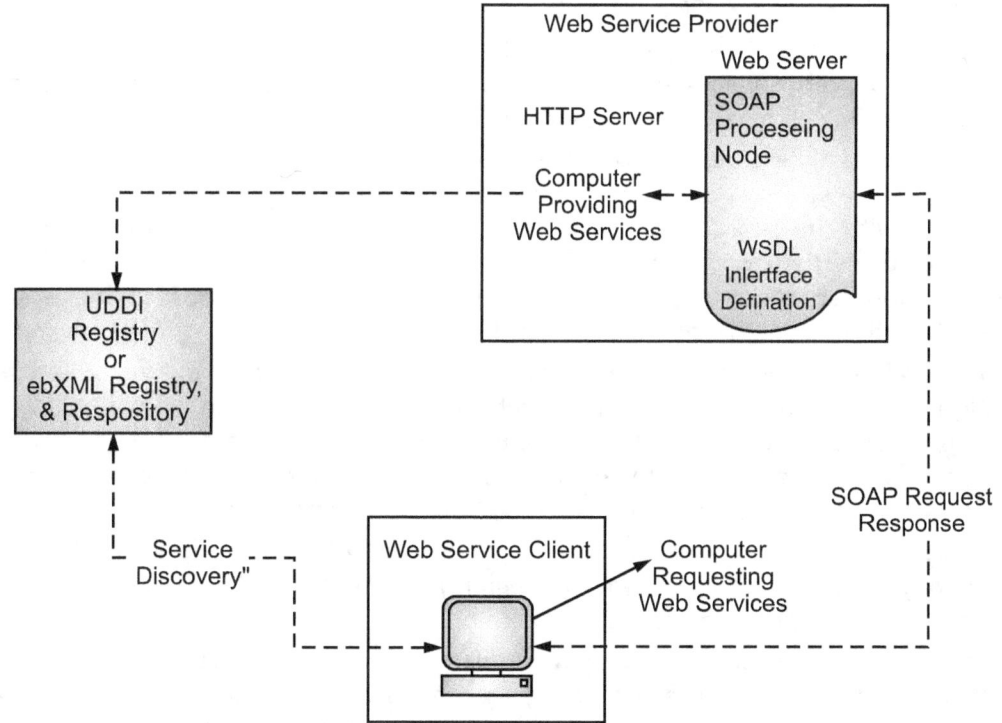

Fig. 5.3 : Working of Web Service

Example

Consider a simple account-management and order processing system. The accounting personnel use a client application built with Visual Basic or JSP to create new accounts and enter new customer orders.

The processing logic for this system is written in Java and resides on a Solaris machine, which also interacts with a database to store information.

The steps to perform this operation are as follows:

- The client program bundles the account registration information into a SOAP message.
- This SOAP message is sent to the web service as the body of an HTTP POST request.
- The web service unpacks the SOAP request and converts it into a command that the application can understand.
- The application processes the information as required and responds with a new unique account number for that customer.
- Next, the web service packages the response into another SOAP message, which it sends back to the client program in response to its HTTP request.
- The client program unpacks the SOAP message to obtain the results of the account registration process.

Characteristics of Web Services

Web services have the following special behavioural characteristics:

- **XML-Based :** Web Services uses XML at data representation and data transportation layers. Using XML eliminates any networking, operating system, or platform binding.
- **Loosely Coupled :** A consumer of a web service is not tied to that web service directly. The web service interface can change over time without compromising the client's ability to interact with the service. A tightly coupled system implies that the client and server logic are closely tied to one another, implying that if one interface changes, the other must be updated. Adopting a loosely coupled architecture tends to make software systems more manageable and allows simpler integration between different systems.
- **Coarse-Grained :** Object-oriented technologies such as Java expose their services through individual methods. An individual method is too fine an operation to provide any useful capability at a corporate level. Building a Java program from scratch requires the creation of several fine-grained methods that are then composed into a coarse-grained service that is consumed by either a client or another service.

  Businesses and the interfaces that they expose should be coarse-grained. Web services technology provides a natural way of defining coarse-grained services that access the right amount of business logic.
- **Ability to be Synchronous or Asynchronous :** Synchronicity refers to the binding of the client to the execution of the service. In synchronous invocations, the client blocks and waits for the service to complete its operation before continuing. Asynchronous operations allow a client to invoke a service and then execute other functions.

Asynchronous clients retrieve their result at a later point in time, while synchronous clients receive their result when the service has completed. Asynchronous capability is a key factor in enabling loosely coupled systems.

- **Supports Remote Procedure Calls (RPCs) :** Web services allow clients to invoke procedures, functions, and methods on remote objects using an XML-based protocol. Remote procedures expose input and output parameters that a web service must support.

  Component development through Enterprise JavaBeans (EJBs) and .NET Components has increasingly become a part of architectures and enterprise deployments over the past couple of years. Both technologies are distributed and accessible through a variety of RPC mechanisms.

  A web service supports RPC by providing services of its own, equivalent to those of a traditional component, or by translating incoming invocations into an invocation of an EJB or a.NET component.

- **Supports Document Exchange :** One of the key advantages of XML is its generic way of representing not only data, but also complex documents. These documents can be as simple as representing a current address, or they can be as complex as representing an entire book or Request for Quotation (RFQ). Web services support the transparent exchange of documents to facilitate business integration.

Benefits of using Web Services

Here are the benefits of using Web Services:

- **Exposing the Existing Function on the network :** A web service is a unit of managed code that can be remotely invoked using HTTP requests. Web services allows you to expose the functionality of your existing code over the network. Once it is exposed on the network, other application can use the functionality of your program.

- **Interoperability :** Web services allow various applications to talk to each other and share data and services among themselves. Other applications can also use the web services. For example, a VB or .NET application can talk to Java web services and vice versa. Web services are used to make the application platform and technology independent.

- **Standardized Protocol :** Web services use standardized industry standard protocol for the communication. All the four layers (Service Transport, XML Messaging, Service Description, and Service Discovery layers) use well-defined protocols in the web services protocol stack. This standardization of protocol stack gives the business many advantages such as a wide range of choices, reduction in the cost due to competition, and increase in the quality.

- **Low Cost of Communication :** Web services use SOAP over HTTP protocol, so you can use your existing low-cost internet for implementing web services. This solution is much less costly compared to proprietary solutions like EDI/B2B. Besides SOAP over HTTP, web services can also be implemented on other reliable transport mechanisms like FTP.

5.2 WSDL, UDDI   [April 2016, Oct. 2016]

WSDL

WSDL is an XML grammar for describing web services. The specification is divided into following major elements:

Definitions:

The definitions element specifies that this document is the HelloService. It also specifies numerous namespaces that will be used throughout the remainder of the document:

<definitions name="HelloService"

. . . .

>

The use of namespaces is important for differentiating elements, and it enables the document to reference multiple external specifications, including the WSDL specification, the SOAP specification, and the XML Schema specification.

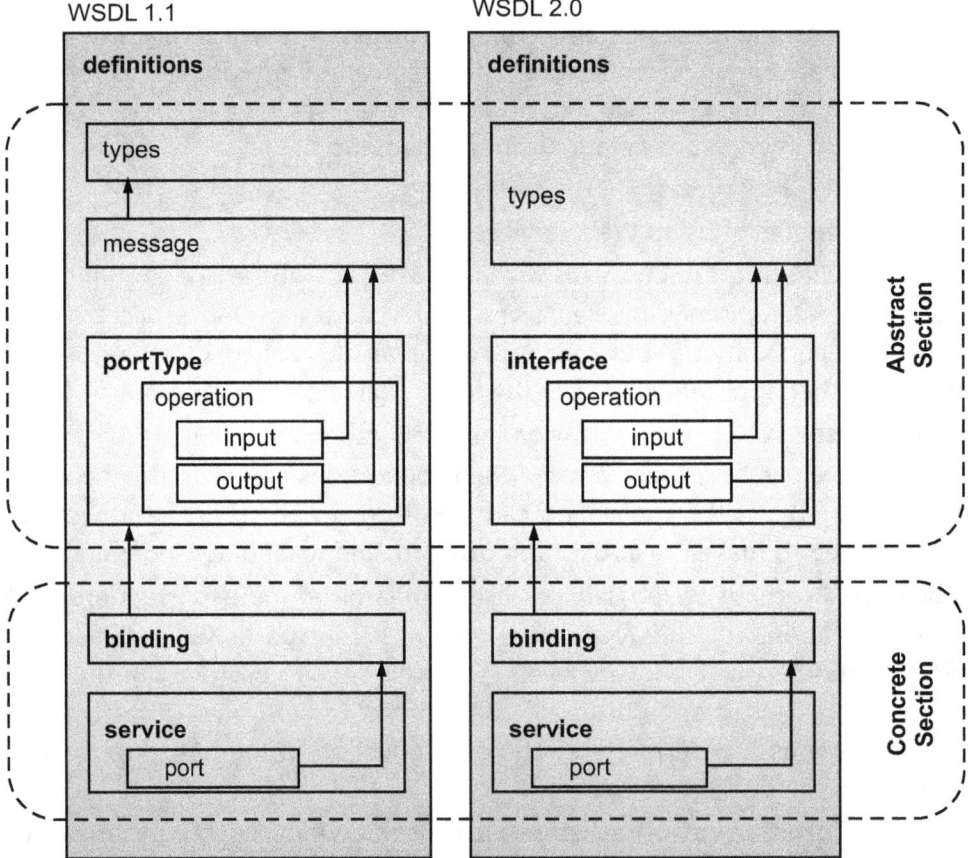

Fig. 5.4 : Representation of concepts defined by WSDL 1.1 and WSDL 2.0 documents

The definitions element also specifies a targetNamespace attribute. The targetNamespace is a convention of XML Schema that enables the WSDL document to refer to itself. In Example, we specified a targetNamespace of http://www.ecerami.com/wsdl/ HelloService.wsdl. However, that the name-space specification does not require that the document actually exist at this location; the important point is that we specify a value that is unique, different from all other namespaces that are defined.

Finally, the definitions element specifies a default namespace :

xmlns= http://schemas.xmlsoap.org/wsdl/. All elements without a namespace prefix, such as message or portType, are therefore assumed to be part of the default WSDL namespace.

Types :

The types element describes all the data types used between the client and server. WSDL is not tied exclusively to a specific typing system, but it uses the W3C XML Schema specification as its default choice. If the service uses only XML Schema built-in simple types, such as strings and integers, the type's element is not required.

Message :

Two message elements are defined. The first represents a request message, SayHelloRequest, and the each of these messages contains a single part element. For the request, the part specifies the function parameters; in this case, we specify a single firstName parameter. For the response, the part specifies the function return values; in this case, we specify a single string return value.

The part element's type attribute specifies an XML Schema data type. The value of the type attribute must be specified as an XML Schema QName-this means that the value of the attribute must be namespace-qualified. For example, the firstNametype attribute is set to xsd:string; the xsd prefix references the namespace for XML Schema, defined earlier within the definitions element. If the function expects multiple arguments or returns multiple values, you can specify multiple part elements.

portType :

The portType element defines a single operation, called sayHello. The operation itself consists of a single input message (SayHelloRequest) and a single output message (SayHelloResponse):

```
<portType name="Hello_PortType">

...

</portType>
```

Much like the type attribute defined earlier, the message attribute must be specified as an XML Schema QName. This means that the value of the attribute must be namespace-qualified. For example, the input element specifies a message attribute of tns:SayHelloRequest; the tns prefix references the targetNamespace defined earlier within the definitions element.

Binding :

The binding element provides specific details on how a portType operation will actually be transmitted over the wire. Bindings can be made available via multiple transports, including HTTP GET, HTTP POST, or SOAP. In fact, we can specify multiple bindings for a single portType.

The binding element itself specifies name and type attributes :

<binding name="Hello_Binding" type="tns:Hello_PortType">

The type attribute references the portType defined earlier in the document. In our case, the binding element therefore references tns:Hello_PortType, defined earlier in the document. The binding element is therefore saying, "I will provide specific details on how the sayHello operation will be transported over the Internet."

SOAP binding:

WSDL 1.1 includes built-in extensions for SOAP 1.1. This enables us to specify SOAP-specific details, including SOAP headers, SOAP encoding styles, and the SOAPAction HTTP header.

Service :

The service element defines the address for invoking the specified service. Most commonly, this includes a URL for invoking the SOAP service.

Input :

Specifies a message format for the request.

Output :

Specifies a message format for the response.

Operation :

An action (method) supported by the service. Each operation consists of input and output messages.

WSDL is a specification defining how to describe web services in a common XML grammar. WSDL describes four critical pieces of data :

- Interface information describing all publicly available functions.
- Data type information for all message requests and message responses.
- Binding information about the transport protocol to be used.
- Address information for locating the specified service.

Using WSDL, a client can locate a web service and invoke any of its publicly available functions. With WSDL-aware tools, we can also automate this process, enabling applications to easily integrate new services with little or no manual code. WSDL therefore, represents a cornerstone of the web service architecture, because it provides a common language for describing services and a platform for automatically integrating those services.

Basic WSDL Example : HelloService.wsdl

Example shows a sample HelloService.wsdl document. The document describes the HelloService.

The service provides a single publicly available function, called *sayHello*. The function expects a single string parameter, and returns a single string. For example, if we pass the parameter world, the service returns, "Hello, world!"

Example : HelloService.wsdl

```xml
<?xml version="1.0" encoding="UTF-8"?>
<definitions name="HelloService"
    targetNamespace="http://www.ecerami.com/wsdl/HelloService.wsdl"
    xmlns="http://schemas.xmlsoap.org/wsdl/"
    xmlns:soap="http://schemas.xmlsoap.org/wsdl/soap/"
    xmlns:tns="http://www.ecerami.com/wsdl/HelloService.wsdl"
    xmlns:xsd=http://www.w3.org/2001/XMLSchema >

    <message name="SayHelloRequest">
        <part name="firstName" type="xsd:string"/>
    </message>
    <message name="SayHelloResponse">
        <part name="greeting" type="xsd:string"/>
    </message>

    <portType name="Hello_PortType">
        <operation name="sayHello">
            <input message="tns:SayHelloRequest"/>
            <output message="tns:SayHelloResponse"/>
        </operation>
    </portType>

    <binding name="Hello_Binding" type="tns:Hello_PortType">
        <soap:binding style="rpc"
                    transport="http://schemas.xmlsoap.org/soap/http"/>
        <operation name="sayHello">
            <soap:operation soapAction="sayHello"/>
            <input>
                <soap:body
```

```
encodingStyle="http://schemas.xmlsoap.org/soap/encoding/"
              namespace="urn:examples:helloservice"
              use="encoded"/>
        </input>
        <output>
          <soap:body
              encodingStyle="http://schemas.xmlsoap.org/soap/encoding/"
              namespace="urn:examples:helloservice"
              use="encoded"/>
        </output>
      </operation>
    </binding>

    <service name="Hello_Service">
      <documentation>WSDL File for HelloService</documentation>
      <port binding="tns:Hello_Binding" name="Hello_Port">
        <soap:address
            location="http://localhost:8080/soap/servlet/rpcrouter"/>
      </port>
    </service>
</definitions>
```

WSDL supports four basic patterns of operation:

1. **One-way:** The service receives a message. The operation therefore has a single input element.
2. **Request-response:** The service receives a message and sends a response. The operation therefore has one input element, followed by one output element To encapsulate errors, an optional fault element can also be specified.
3. **Solicit-response:** The service sends a message and receives a response. The operation therefore has one output element, followed by one input element. To encapsulate errors, an optional fault element can also be specified.
4. **Notification:** The service sends a message. The operation therefore has a single output element.

The request-response pattern is most commonly used in SOAP services.

UDDI

UDDI (Universal Description, Discovery, and Integration) is an XML-based registry for businesses worldwide to list themselves on the Internet.

UDDI currently represents the discovery layer within the web service protocol stack. UDDI was originally created by Microsoft, IBM, and Ariba, and represents a technical specification for publishing and finding businesses and web services.

At its core, UDDI consists of two parts. First, UDDI is a technical specification for building a distributed directory of businesses and web services. Data is stored within a specific XML format. The UDDI specification includes API details for searching existing data and publishing new data. Second, the UDDI Business Registry is a fully operational implementation of the UDDI specification. Launched in May 2001 by Microsoft and IBM, the UDDI registry now enables anyone to search existing UDDI data. It also enables any company to register itself and its services.

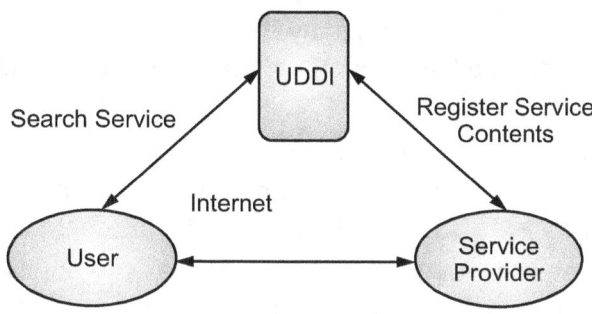

Fig. 5.5: UDDI

UDDI Technical Architecture

Private UDDI Registries : As an alternative to using the public federated network of UDDI registries available on the Internet, companies or industry groups may choose to implement their own private UDDI registries.

These exclusive services are designed for the sole purpose of allowing members of the company or of the industry group to share and advertise services amongst themselves.

Regardless of whether the UDDI registry is a part of the global federated network or a privately owned and operated registry, the one thing that ties them all together is a common web services API for publishing and locating businesses and services advertised within the UDDI registry.

Features of UDDI:

- Platform independent
- Built into the Microsoft .NET platform
- XML-based
- Supports all major platforms and software providers like IBM, Intel, Microsoft, Oracle, HP and Sun
- Described by WSDL
- Over 250 companies are members of the UDDI community

Working of UDDI:

The most important part of the UDDI project is business registration. Business registration includes submission of an XML file that describes the business and its web services.

UDDI is compared to a telephone directory book it can be classified in the three components.

1. **White pages** includes the address, contact and known identifiers. It contain :
    *   Basic information about the company and its business.
    *   Basic contact information including business name, address, contact phone number, etc.
    *   A Unique identifiers for the company tax IDs. This information allows others to discover your web service based upon your business identification.

2. **Yellow pages**
    *   Yellow pages include the industrial category information. It contains more details about the company. They include descriptions of the kind of electronic capabilities the company can offer to anyone who wants to do business with it.
    *   Yellow pages uses commonly accepted industrial categorization schemes, industry codes, product codes, business identification codes and the like to make it easier for companies to search through the listings and find exactly what they want.

3. **Green pages**

Green pages contain technical information about a web service. A green page allows someone to bind to a Web service after it's been found. It includes:
    *   The various interfaces
    *   The URL locations
    *   Discovery information and similar data required to find and run the Web service

UDDI is not restricted to describing web services based on SOAP. Rather, UDDI can be used to describe any service, from a single webpage or email address all the way up to SOAP, CORBA, and Java RMI services.

UDDI Technical Architecture

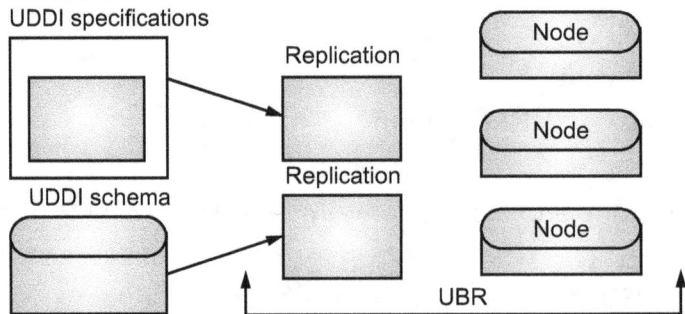

Fig 5.6: UDDI Technical Architecture

UBR

The UDDI Business Registry (UBR), (also known as the Public Cloud) is a conceptually single system built from multiple nodes that has their data synchronized through replication.

The UDDI technical architecture consists of three parts:

1. UDDI data model: This is an XML Schema for describing businesses and web services.

UDDI includes an XML Schema that describes five data structures:

- Business Entity
- Business Service
- Binding Template
- tModel
- Publisher Assertion

2. UDDI API Specification: This is a specification of API for searching and publishing UDDI data.

A Specification of API for searching and publishing UDDI data. The specifications include:

- **UDDI Replication:** Its describe the data replication processes and also describe the interfaces. These interfaces are registry operator to conform achieving data replication among sites.
- **UDDI Operators:** This document outlines the behavior and operational parameters.
- **UDDI Programmer's API:** This specification inquiring about services hosted in a registry.
- **UDDI Data Structures:** Specification of XML structures contained within the SOAP messages.

3. UDDI cloud services: This consists of operator sites that provide implementations of the UDDI specification and synchronize all data on a scheduled basis.

- The current cloud services provide a logically centralized, but physically distributed, directory. This means that data submitted to one root node will automatically be replicated across all the other root nodes. Currently, data replication occurs every 24 hours.
- UDDI cloud services are currently provided by Microsoft and IBM.
- It is also possible to set up private UDDI registries. For example, a large company may set up its own private UDDI registry for registering all internal

Web services: As these registries are not automatically synchronized with the root

UDDI nodes, they are not considered part of the UDDI cloud.

Registering WSDL with the UDDI Registry

How can we register WSDL with the UDDI registry? UDDI aims at a generic means to publish and find information on services. This indicates that UDDI is independent of any particular protocols, such as SOAP, and any services description language, such as WSDL. Accordingly, there is no description of the registration of WSDL. Instead, we show an approach as a best practice.

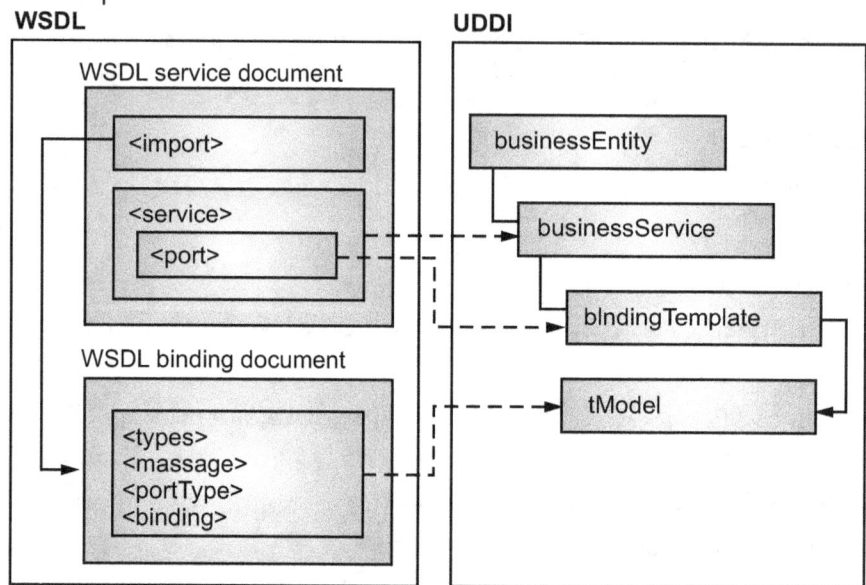

Fig 5.7 : Registering WSDL with UDDI registry

Fig. 5.7 shows how the interface and implementation parts of WSDL documents are integrated into UDDI. The implementation part refers to the interface part with the import element on the WSDL side. On the UDDI side, Binding Template refers to TModel with the tModel key, as in the UDDI specification.

5.3 Introduction to SOAP XML-PRC   [April 2016, Oct. 2016]

SOAP (Simple Object Access Protocol) is a protocol specification for exchanging structured information in the implementation of Web Services in computer networks. It is a way for a program running in one kind of an operating system (such as Linux) to communicate with a program in the same or another kind of an operating system (such as Windows) by using the HTTP and its XML as the mechanisms for information exchange. It relies on XML for its message format, and usually relies on other Application Layer protocols, most notably Remote Procedure Call (RPC) and for message negotiation and transmission.

SOAP can form the foundation layer of a web services protocol stack, providing a basic messaging framework upon which web services can be built. This XML based protocol consists of three parts:

- An **envelope**, which defines what is in the message and how to process it
- A **set of encoding** rules for expressing instances of application-defined data types
- A **convention** for representing procedure calls and responses

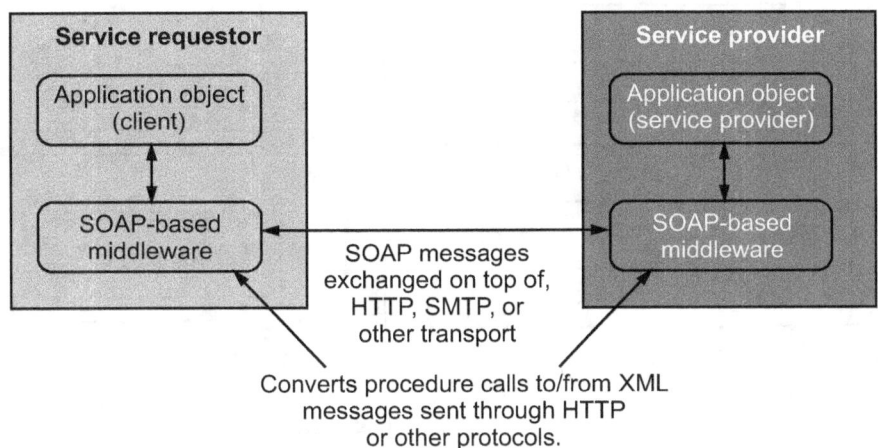

Fig 5.8 : SOAP

A SOAP message could be sent to a web-service-enabled web site.

For example, a real-estate price database, with the parameters needed for a search. The site would then return an XML-formatted document with the resulting data e.g., prices, location, features. Because the data is returned in a standardized machine-parseable format, it could then be integrated directly into a third-party web site or application.

The SOAP architecture consists of several layers of specifications: for message format, Message Exchange Patterns (MEP), underlying transport protocol bindings, message processing models, and protocol extensibility.

SOAP is the successor of XML-RPC, though it borrows its transport and interaction neutrality and the envelope/header/body from elsewhere (probably from WDDX).

The SOAP specification defines the messaging framework which consists of:

- The SOAP processing model defining the rules for processing a SOAP message.
- The SOAP extensibility model defining the concepts of SOAP features and SOAP modules.
- The SOAP underlying protocol binding framework describing the rules for defining a binding to an underlying protocol that can be used for exchanging SOAP messages between SOAP nodes.
- The SOAP message construct defining the structure of a SOAP message.

SOAP Message :

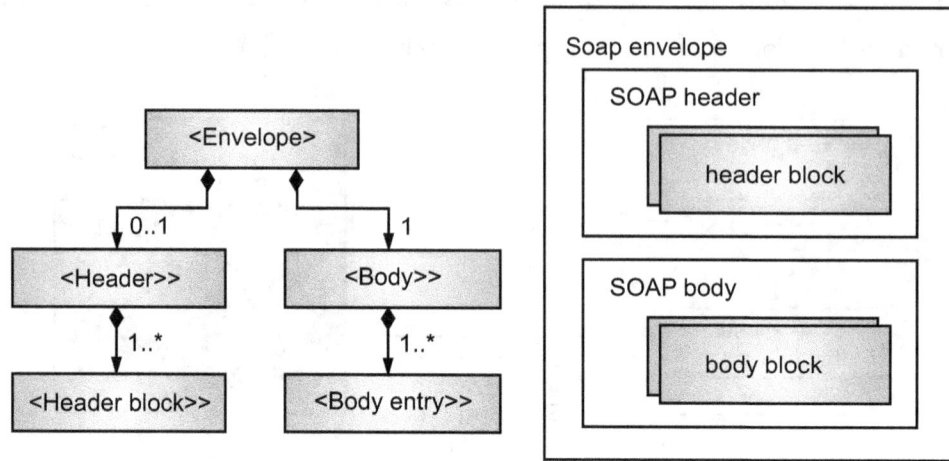

Fig 5.9 : SOAP Messaging

SOAP is based on message exchanges :

- Messages are seen as envelopes where the application encloses the data to be sent.

- A SOAP message consists of a SOAP of an <Envelope> element containing an optional <Header> and a mandatory <Body> element.

- The contents of these elements are SOAP envelope application defined and not a part of the SOAP specifications.

- A SOAP <Header> contains blocks of SOAP header. All immediate child elements of the Header element are called Header Blocks. A header block is identified by its fully qualified element name, which consists of the namespace URI and the local name.

- The SOAP <Body> is where the main end to-end information conveyed in a SOAP message must be carried.

Sample SOAP message :

POST /InStock HTTP/1.1

Host: www.example.org

Content-Type: application/soap+xml; charset=utf-8

Content-Length: nnn

```
<?xml version="1.0"?>
<soap:Envelope xmlns:soap="http://www.w3.org/2003/05/soap-envelope">
  <soap:Header>
  </soap:Header>
```

```
<soap:Body>

  <m:GetStockPrice xmlns:m="http://www.example.org/stock">

    <m:StockName>IBM</m:StockName>

  </m:GetStockPrice>

</soap:Body>

</soap:Envelope>
```

Advantages :

- SOAP is versatile enough to allow for the use of different transport protocols. The standard stacks use HTTP as a transport protocol, but other protocols are also usable (e.g. SMTP).

- Since the SOAP model is good in the HTTP get/response model, it can tunnel easily over existing firewalls and proxies, without modifications to the SOAP protocol, and can use the existing infrastructure.

Disadvantages :

- Because of the verbose XML format, SOAP can be considerably slower than competing middleware technologies such as CORBA (Common Object Request Broker Architecture). This may not be an issue when only small messages are sent. To improve performance for the special case of XML with embedded binary objects, the Message Transmission Optimization Mechanism was introduced.

- When relying on HTTP as a transport protocol and not using WS-Addressing   the roles of the interacting client are fixed. Only one   client can use the services of the other.

XML-RPC: **[Oct. 2016]**

XML-RPC is a simple protocol for carrying out Remote Procedure Calls (RPC) over TCP/IP. It uses two standards of the internet, Hypertext Transfer Protocol (HTTP) and eXtensible Markup Language (XML) to create a standard way of calling remote web services and receiving a response. XML-RPC is among the simplest and most foolproof web service approaches that make it easy for computers to call procedures on other computers.

Why to use XML-RPC?

If you need to integrate multiple computing environments, but don't need to share complex data structure directly, you will find that XML-RPC lets you establish communications quickly and easily.

Even if you work within a single environment, you may find that the RPC approach makes it easy to connect programs that have different data models or processing expectations and that it can provide easy access to reusable logic.

- XML-RPC is an excellent tool for establishing a wide variety of connections between computers.

- XML-RPC offers integrators an opportunity to use a standard vocabulary and approach for exchanging information.

- XML-RPC's most obvious field of application is connecting different kinds of environments, allowing PHP to talk with Perl, Python, ASP, and so on.

XML-RPC Technical Overview

XML-RPC consists of three relatively small parts:

- **XML-RPC Data Model:** A set of types for use in passing parameters, return values, and faults (error messages).

- **XML-RPC Request Structures:** An HTTP POST request containing method and parameter information.

- **XML-RPC Response Structures:** An HTTP response that contains return values or fault information.

XML-RPC Conversation

Remote Procedure Calls (RPC) is not a new concept. A client/server system, RPCs have traditionally been procedures called in a program on one machine that go over the network to some RPC server that actually implements the called procedure. The RPC server bundles up the results of the procedure and sends those results back to the caller. The calling program then continues executing. While this system requires a lot of overhead and latency, it also allows less powerful machines to access high powered resources. It also allows applications to harness the computational muscle of a network of machines.

Dave Winer, of Frontier and Userland fame, helped extend the concept of RPC with XML and HTTP. XML-RPC works by:

- Encoding the RPC requests into XML and sending them over a standard HTTP connection to a server or listener piece.

- The listener decodes the XML, executes the requested procedure, and then packages up the results in XML and sends them back over the wire to the client.

- The client decodes the XML, converts the results into standard language data types, and continues executing. Figure 1 is a diagram showing an actual XML-RPC conversation between a client (requesting the get_account_info RPC) and a listener who is returning the results of that procedure.

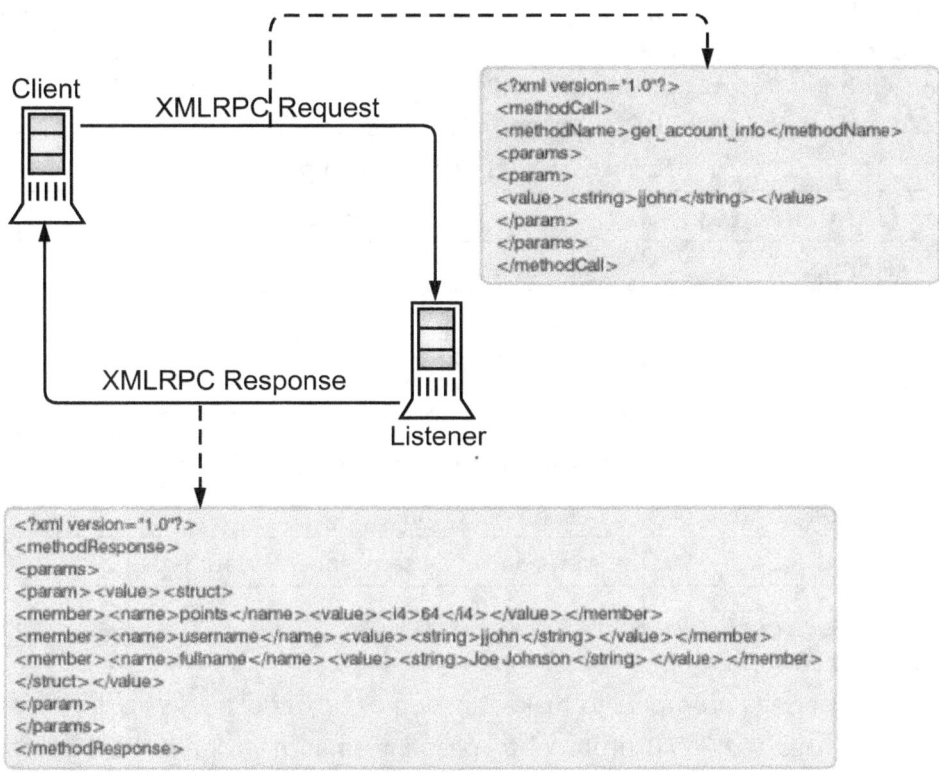

Fig 5.10 : Sample XML-RPC Conversation

XML-RPC can cross programming language and operating system platforms, allowing clients and servers written in different languages to work together. Perl clients can talk to Java servers; Python listeners can service PHP requests; you can even write XML-RPC programs in bad, old C. XML-RPC is extremely easy to work with because the details of the XML translations are hidden from the user, unless, of course, you are implementing your own XML-RPC library.

There are two important aspects of this protocol that you should keep in mind when building your middleware.

1. XML-RPC is built on HTTP and like ordinary web traffic; its stateless conversations are of the request and response variety. There is no built-in support for transactions or encryption.

2. The other important detail to remember is that XML-RPC has a finite set of data types. Client procedure arguments and listener return values are mapped in a non-extendable XML subset. In practice, though, XML-RPC's datatypes are often flexible enough to do complex tasks.

Table 5.1 lists all the XML-RPC data types. Four of these are used far more than the others. For single value datatypes, <sting> and <int>, which respectively denote string and integer data, are the hard working for most XML-RPC programs.

There are also two kinds of collection data types. Simple sequences of arbitrary data types are represented with the <array> tag. Records, structures, and associative arrays are represented with the <struct> tag. XML-RPC structures are formed with key-value pairs, which should feel natural to Perl, Python, and PHP coders.

Table 5.1: XML-RPC data types

XML-RPC tag	Description
<string>	a sequence of characters
<int>	signed or unsigned 32-bit integer values
<boolean>	true(1) or false(0)
<double>	signed double precision floating point numbers
<dateTime.iso8601>	date and time (but no time zone)
<base64>	a base64 encoded string
<array>	a container for a sequence of data types
<struct>	a container for key-value pairs

Characteristics of XML-RPC

- XML-RPC permits programs to make function or procedure calls across a network.
- XML-RPC uses the HTTP protocol to pass information from a client computer to a server computer.
- XML-RPC uses a small XML vocabulary to describe the nature of requests and responses.
- XML-RPC client specifies a procedure name and parameters in the XML request, and the server returns either a fault or a response in the XML response.
- XML-RPC parameters are a simple list of types and content - structs and arrays are the most complex types available.
- XML-RPC has no notion of objects and no mechanism for including information that uses other XML vocabulary.
- With XML-RPC and web services, however, the web becomes a collection of procedural connections where computers exchange information along tightly bound paths.
- XML-RPC emerged in early 1998; it was published by UserLand Software and initially implemented in their Frontier product.

Representational State Transfer (REST):

REST attempts to describe architectures which use HTTP or similar protocols by constraining the interface to a set of well-known, standard operations (like GET, POST, PUT, DELETE for HTTP). Here, the focus is on interacting with stateful resources, rather than messages or operations.

An architecture based on REST (one that is 'RESTful') can use WSDL to describe SOAP messaging over HTTP, can be implemented as an abstraction purely on top of SOAP (e.g., WS-Transfer), or can be created without using SOAP at all.

WSDL offers support for binding to all the HTTP request methods (not only GET and POST) so it enables a better implementation of RESTful Web services. However, support for this specification is still poor in software development kits, which often offer tools only for WSDL

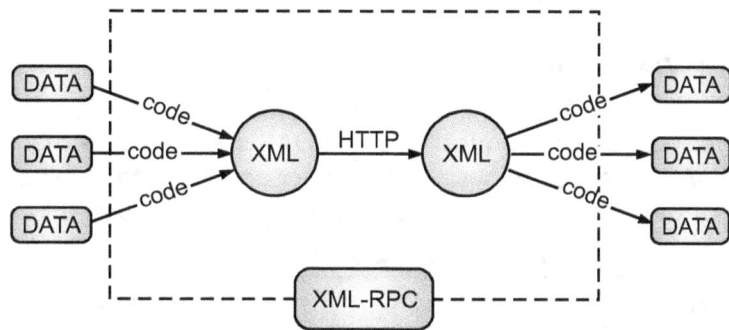

Fig. 5.11 : Representational State Transfer

Creating and Calling Web Service:

The two main components of an XML-RPC "message" are **methods** and **parameters**. Methods correspond loosely to the functions we define in PHP, while parameters correspond to the variables we pass to those functions. Parameters can be one of a number of different types, such as strings, integers and arrays - very similar to the variable used to in PHP. In addition, XML-RPC defines other tags for things like error handling

An XML-RPC "conversation", between two systems begins with a **request** from the XML-RPC client, which the server answers with a response. The request contains a method and perhaps some parameters required by the method. The response replies with parameters that contain the requested data. The process is very much like using a function in a PHP script; we call a function and pass it some variables. The function then responds by returning some variables.

Creating and Calling web services

A web service consists of a server to serve requests to the web service and a client to invoke methods on the web service. The PHP class library provides the SOAP extension to develop SOAP servers and clients and the XML-RPC extension to create XML-RPC servers and clients.

1. Installing the PHP Web Services Extensions:

The SOAP and XML-RPC extensions are packaged with the PHP 5 installation. The SOAP extension and the XML-RPC extension are not enabled by default in a PHP installation. To enable the SOAP and XML-RPC extensions, add the following extension directives in the php.ini configuration file.

[soap]; Enables or disables WSDL caching feature.

soap.wsdl_cache_enabled=1 ; Sets the directory name where SOAP extension will put cache files.

soap.wsdl_cache_dir="/tmp"; (time to live) Sets the number of seconds while cached file will be used; instead of original one.

soap.wsdl_cache_ttl=86400

When developing a Web Service and maybe changing the WSDL, this is, of course, a no-brainer. Therefore, set soap.wsdl_cache_enabled to off during development, but turn it on production servers. Restart the Apache 2 server to activate the SOAP and XML-RPC extensions. The SOAP extension supports subsets of the SOAP 1.1, SOAP 1.2, and WSDL 1.1 specifications.

2. Creating a SOAP Web Service:

A SOAP server and a SOAP client may be created using the SOAP PHP class library. A SOAP server serves web service requests and a SOAP client invokes methods on the SOAP web service. The SOAP library provides various functions for creating a SOAP server and a SOAP client. Some of the commonly used SOAP functions are discussed in Table 5.1.

Table 5.2 : SOAP functions

Method	Description
SoapServer->__construct(mixed wsdl [, array options])	Creates a SoapServer object. The wsdl parameter specifies the URI of the WSDL. SoapServer options such as SOAP version may be specified in the options array.
SoapServer->addFunction(mixed functions)	Adds one or more PHP functions that will handle SOAP requests. A single function may be added as a string. More than one function may be added as an array.
SoapServer->fault()	SoapServer fault indicating an error.
SoapServer->getFunctions()	Returns a list of functions.
SoapServer->handle()	Processes a SOAP request, invokes required functions and sends back a response.
SoapServer->setClass(string class_name [, mixed args [, mixed ...]])	Sets the class that will handle SOAP requests. Exports all methods from the specified class. The args are used by the default class constructor.
SoapHeader->__construct()	Creates a SOAP header.
SoapClient->__soapCall(string function_name, array arguments [, array options [, mixed input_headers [, array & output_headers]]])	Invokes a SOAP function.
SoapClient->__doRequest()	Performs a SOAP request.
SoapClient->__getFunctions()	Returns a list of SOAP functions.
SoapClient->__getTypes()	Returns a list of SOAP types.

3. Creating a SOAP Server :

Before we create a SOAP server, we need to create a WSDL document defining the web service. The WSDL document defines the operations that the web service provides. We will create an example web service that provides an operation getCatalogEntry, which returns a catalog entry for a catalog ID. A WSDL is an XML document in the http://schemas.xmlsoap.org/wsdl/ namespace. Some of the elements of a WSDL are discussed 5.2

Next, create a WSDL document for the example web service. The example WSDL document, catalog.wsdl, defines message elements getCatalogRequest and getCatalog Response for the request and response messages. In the WSDL document, define a portType, CatalogPortType, for the getCatalogEntry operation that returns a catalog entry as a HTML string for a string catalogId. Define a binding, CatalogBinding, for the getCatalogEntry operation and the input output messages.

The soap:binding element specifies that the binding is bound to the SOAP protocol format.

The soap:operation element specifies information for the operation.

The soap:body element specifies how the message parts appear inside the SOAP Body element. Define a service CatalogService that consists of a port, CatalogPort, which is associated with the CatalogBinding binding. The soap:address element specifies the URI of an address. The catalog.wsdl WSDL document is listed below.

```
<?xml version ='1.0' encoding ='UTF-8' ?>
<definitions name='Catalog'
  targetNamespace='http://example.org/catalog'
  xmlns:tns=' http://example.org/catalog '
  xmlns:soap='http://schemas.xmlsoap.org/wsdl/soap/'
  xmlns:xsd='http://www.w3.org/2001/XMLSchema'
  xmlns:soapenc='http://schemas.xmlsoap.org/soap/
  encoding/'
  xmlns:wsdl='http://schemas.xmlsoap.org/wsdl/'
  xmlns='http://schemas.xmlsoap.org/wsdl/'>

<message name='getCatalogRequest'>
  <part name='catalogId' type='xsd:string'/>
</message>
<message name='getCatalogResponse'>
  <part name='Result' type='xsd:string'/>
</message>
```

```
<portType name='CatalogPortType'>
  <operation name='getCatalogEntry'>
    <input message='tns:getCatalogRequest'/>
    <output message='tns:getCatalogResponse'/>
  </operation>
</portType>

<binding name='CatalogBinding' type=
'tns:CatalogPortType'>
  <soap:binding style='rpc'
    transport='http://schemas.xmlsoap.org/soap/http'
  />
  <operation name='getCatalogEntry'>
    <soap:operation soapAction='urn:localhost-catalog#
    getCatalogEntry'/>
    <input>
      <soap:body use='encoded' namespace=
      'urn:localhost-catalog'
        encodingStyle='http://schemas.xmlsoap.org/soap
       /encoding/'/>
    </input>
    <output>
      <soap:body use='encoded' namespace=
    'urn:localhost-catalog'
        encodingStyle='http://schemas.xmlsoap.org/soap/
    encoding/'/>
    </output>
  </operation>
</binding>

<service name='CatalogService'>
  <port name='CatalogPort' binding=
  'CatalogBinding'>
    <soap:address location='http://localhost/soap-server.php'/>
  </port>
</service>
</definitions>
```

Copy the catalog.wsdl document to, the directory in which PHP scripts are run. Create a PHP script, soap-server.php, to define the operations provided by the CatalogService web service.

The soap-server.php script is listed below.

```php
<?php
function getCatalogEntry($catalogId)
{
  if($catalogId=='catalog1')

return "<HTML>
 <HEAD>
  <TITLE>Catalog</TITLE>
 </HEAD>
 <BODY>
<p> </p>
 <table border>
<tr><th>CatalogId</th>
<th>Journal</th><th>Section
</th><th>Edition</th><th>
Title</th><th>Author</th>
</tr><tr><td>catalog1</td>
<td> Computer </td><td>
XML</td><td>Dec2010</td>
<td>JAXP validation</td>
<td>Mangesh</td></tr>
</table>
</BODY>
</HTML>";
elseif ($catalogId='catalog2')
return "<HTML>
 <HEAD>
  <TITLE>Catalog</TITLE>
 </HEAD>
 <BODY>
<p> </p>
 <table border>
```

```
<tr><th>CatalogId</th><th>
Journal</th><th>Section</th>
<th>Edition</th><th>Title
</th><th>Author
</th></tr><tr><td>catalog1
</td><td> Electronics </td>
<td>XML</td><td>July 2006</td>
<td>The Java XPath API
</td><td>Elliotte Harold</td>
</tr>
</table>
</BODY>
</HTML>";
}


ini_set("soap.wsdl_cache_enabled", "0");
$server = new SoapServer("catalog.wsdl");
$server->addFunction("getCatalogEntry");
$server->handle();


?>
```

In the soap-server.php script, define a function getCatalogEntry() that takes a catalogId as an argument and returns a string consisting of an HTML document. The HTML document string returned comprises of the catalog entry for the specified catalogId.

```
function getCatalogEntry($catalogId)
{
  if($catalogId=='catalog1')
          return "<HTML> ... </HTML>";
elseif ($catalogId='catalog2')
return "<HTML>...</HTML>";
}
```

The WSDL cache is enabled by default. Disable the WSDL cache by setting the soap.wsdl_cache_enabled configuration option to 0.

ini_set("soap.wsdl_cache_enabled", "0");

Create a SoapServer object using the catalog.wsdl WSDL.

$server = new SoapServer("catalog.wsdl");

Add the getCatalogEntry function to the SoapServer object using the addFunction() method. The SOAP web service provides the getCatalogEntry operation.

$server->addFunction("getCatalogEntry");

Handle a SOAP request.

$server->handle();

We will create a SOAP client to send a request to the SOAP server.

4. Creating a SOAP Client :

Create a PHP script, soap-client.php, In the PHP script, create a SOAP client using the SoapClient class. The WSDL document, catalog.wsdl, is specified as an argument to the SoapClient constructor.

The soap-client.php script is listed below.

```php
<?php
    $client = new SoapClient("catalog.wsdl");
    $catalogId='catalog1';
    $response = $client->getCatalogEntry($catalogId);
    echo $response;
?>
```

The WSDL document specifies the operations that are available to the SOAP client.

$client = new SoapClient("catalog.wsdl");

Specify the catalogId for which a catalog entry is to be retrieved. Invoke the getCatalogEntry method of the SOAP web service.

$catalogId='catalog1';

$response = $client->getCatalogEntry($catalogId);

Output the response to the browser.

echo $response;

Call the soap-client.php PHP script with the URL http://localhost/soap-client.php.The catalog entry for the catalog1 catalogId gets output as shown in Table 5.3.

Table 5.3 : After_Calling the SOAP client

CatalogID	Journal	Section	Edition	Title	Author
Catalog1	Computer	XML	Dec 2010	JAXP validation	Mangesh

5. Creating an XML-RPC Web Service

XML-RPC is a specification and a set of implementations designed for applications to make remote procedure calls over the network. The remote procedure calls are made using HTTP as the transport and XML as the encoding.

Structure of an XML-RPC Request and Response

An XML-RPC message is an HTTP-POST request. The request body is in XML format. The request is sent to an XML-RPC server, which runs some business logic and returns a response in the form of XML. An example XML-RPC request is listed below.

```
POST /php/xmlrpc-server.php HTTP/1.0
User-Agent: Example Client
Host: localhost
Content-Type: text/xml
Content-length: 190
```

```xml
<?xml version="1.0"?>
<methodCall>
    <methodName>getCatalog</methodName>
    <params>
       <param>
          <value><string>catalog1
          </string></value>
          </param>
       </params>
    </methodCall>
```

The URL in the header, /php/xmlrpc-server.php specifies the server URL to which the request is sent. The HTTP version is also specified. The User-Agent and Host are required to be specified. The Content-Type is text/xml and the Content-Length specifies the content length.

The request body is in XML with root element as methodCall. The methodCall element is required to contain a sub-element methodName which specifies the name of the method to be invoked as a string. If the XML-RPC request has parameters, the methodCall element contains sub-element params. The params element contains one or more param elements. Each of the param elements contains a value element. The param value may be specified as a string, a Boolean, a four-byte signed integer, double-precision signed, floating point number, date/time, or base-64 encoded binary. The sub-element of value in which a param value is specified is different for different value types. If a type is not specified the default type is string. The sub-elements for the value types are listed in Table 5.4.

Table 5.4 : Value Elements

Value Type	Element
ASCII String	<string>
Four-byte signed integer	<i4> or <int>
Boolean	<boolean>
Double-precision signed or floating point number	<double>
Date/time	<dateTime.iso8601>
Base-64 encoded binary	<base64>

A param value may also be of type <struct>. A <struct> element consists of <member> elements. Each <member> element contains a <name> element and a <value> element. An example of struct value is listed below.

```
<struct>
    <member>
        <name>catalogId</name>
        <value><string>catalog1
        </string></value>
    </member>
    <member>
        <name>journal</name>
        <value><string>IBM developerWorks
        </string></value>
    </member>
</struct>
```

A value element in a member element may be of any of the param data types including struct. A param type may also be of type <array>. An <array> element consists of a <data> element, which consists of one or more <value> elements. An example of an <array> param value is listed below.

```
<array>
    <data>
        <value><i4>1</i4></value>
        <value><string>IBM developerWorks
        </string></value>
        <value>XML</value>
        <value><string>Introduction to dom4j
        </string></value>
        <value><string>Akash</string
        ></value>
    </data>
</array>
```

A <value> element in a <data> element may consist of any of the data types including struct and array. The server response to an XML-RPC request is in the format of XML. An example response is listed below.

HTTP/1.1 200 OK

Connection: close

Content-Length: 190

Content-Type: text/xml

Date:

Server: Example Server

```
<?xml version="1.0"?>
<methodResponse>
    <params>
        <param>
            <value><string>Introduction
            to SQLXML</string></value>
            </param>
        </params>
    </methodResponse>
```

If an error has not occurred, the server response returns "200 OK." The Connection Header specifies the state of the connection after the response is completed. For non-persistent connection, the Connection Header value is "close." The Content-Type is text/xml. The response body is in XML format with root element as methodResponse. The methodResponse element consists of a single <params> element, which consists of a single <param> element. The <param> element contains a single <value> element.

Instead of a <params> element a methodResponse element may also consists of a single <fault> element. The <fault> element contains a <value> element, which contains a <struct> element with two <member> elements faultCode of type integer and faultString of type string. An example of a XML-RPC server response with a <<fault> element is listed below.

HTTP/1.1 200 OK

Connection: close

Content-Length: 190

Content-Type: text/xml

Date:

Server: Example Server

```
<?xml version="1.0"?>
<methodResponse>
    <fault>
        <value>
```

```
<struct>
    <member>
        <name>faultCode</name>
        <value><int>4</int
        ></value>
        </member>
    <member>
        <name>faultString</name>
        <value><string>No such Method.
        </string></value>
        </member>
    </struct>
    </value>
    </fault>
</methodResponse>
```

6. Creating an XML-RPC Server

The PHP XML-RPC extension is a PHP implementation of the XML-RPC specification. The XML-RPC PHP class library provides functions to create a XML-RPC server and invoke methods on the server. Some of the commonly used XML-RPC functions are given in Table 5.5.

Table 5.5 : XML-RPC PHP Functions

Function	Description
xmlrpc_server_create ()	Creates an XML-RPC server.
xmlrpc_encode_request (string method, mixed params [, array output_options])	Generates XML for a method request or response. Returns a string or FALSE on error.
xmlrpc_encode (mixed value)	Generates XML for a PHP variable.
xmlrpc_decode_request (string xml, string &method [, string encoding])	Decodes XML into PHP. Returns an array.
xmlrpc_get_type (mixed value)	Returns XML-RPC data types, for example "struct", "int", "string", "base64" for a PHP value.
xmlrpc_set_type (string &value, string type)	Sets xmlrpc type, base64, or datetime for a PHP string value. Returns True or False on error.
xmlrpc_server_register_method (resource server, string method_name, string function)	Registers PHP function to a web service method. The method_name value is the same as the value of the methodName element in the XML-RPC request.

... (Contd.)

Function	Description
xmlrpc_server_call_method (resource server, string xml, mixed user_data [, array output_options])	Parses XML request and invokes method. Returns result of method call. The user_data parameter specifies any application data for the method handler function. The output_options parameter specifies a hashed array of options for generating response XML. The following options may be specified. output_type: Specifies output data type; "php" or "xml". Default data type is "xml". If output type is "php" other values are ignored. verbosity: Specifies compactness of generated message.escaping: Specifies if and how to escape some characters.version: Specifies version of XML to use. Value may be "xmlrpc", "soap 1.1" and "simple". Version may also be set to "auto", which specifies to use the version the request came in. encoding: Specifies the encoding of the data. Default is "iso-8859-1".Example value of the output_options parameter is as follows.$output_options = array("output_type" => "xml", "verbosity" => "no_white_space", "escaping" => array("markup", "non-ascii", "non-print"), "version" => "xmlrpc", "encoding" => "utf-8");
xmlrpc_is_fault (array arg)	Determines if an array value represents XML-RPC fault.
xmlrpc_server_destroy (resource server)	Destroys a server resource.

Create a PHP script, xmlrpc-webservice.php. In the PHP script, define a function, hello_func. Any function that is call by a client is required to take three parameters: the first parameter is the name of the XML-RPC method invoked. The second parameter is an array containing the parameters sent by the client. The third parameter is the application data sent in the user_data parameter of the xmlrpc_server_call_method() function. In the hello_func function, retrieve the first parameter, which is a name sent by the client, and output a Hello message.

```
function hello_func($method_name, $params, $app_data)
{
$name = $params[0];
return "Hello $name.";
}
```

Create an XML-RPC server using the xmlrpc_server_create() method.

```
$xmlrpc_server=xmlrpc_server_create();
```

If a server does not get created, the xmlrpc_server_create method returns FALSE. Register the hello_func function with the server using the xmlrpc_server_register_method method. The first argument to the xmlrpc_server_register_method method is the XML-RPC server resource. The second argument is name of the method that is provided by the web service, which is the <methodName> element value in a XML-RPC request. The third argument is the PHP function to be registered with the server.

```
$registered=xmlrpc_server_register_method
($xmlrpc_server, "hello", "hello_func" );
```

If the PHP function gets registered, the xmlrpc_server_register_method returns TRUE.

7. Creating an XML-RPC Client :

We will create a XML-RPC client to send a request to the XML-RPC server. First, specify the XML string to be sent in the request.

The PHP script, xmlrpc-webservice.php

```
<?php
function hello_func($method_name, $params, $app_data)
{
$name = $params[0];
return "Hello $name.";
}
$xmlrpc_server=xmlrpc_server_create();
$registered=xmlrpc_server_register_method
($xmlrpc_server, "hello", "hello_func" );
$request_xml = <<< END
<?xml version="1.0"?>
<methodCall>
    <methodName>hello</methodName>
        <params>
          <param>
            <value>
```

```
                <string>Akash</string>
            </value>
          </param>
        </params>
</methodCall>
END;
$response=xmlrpc_server_call_method( $xmlrpc_server,
$request_xml, '', array(output_type => "xml"));
print $response;// Output the XML-RPC response from the server.
?>
```

To escape XML in PHP, <<<END ....END; is used. An XML document demarker other END may also be used. The methodCall element specifies the web service method that is to be invoked. Invoke the web service method using the xmlrpc_server_call_method function. The first argument to the xmlrpc_server_call_method function is the server resource. The second argument is the string containing the XML-RPC request. The third argument is the application data that is sent to the third parameter of the method handler function.

Copy the xmlrpc-webservice.php script in the directory. Invoke the PHP script with the URL http://localhost/xmlrpc-webservice.php. The response from the server gets output to the browser as shown in Fig. 5.12.

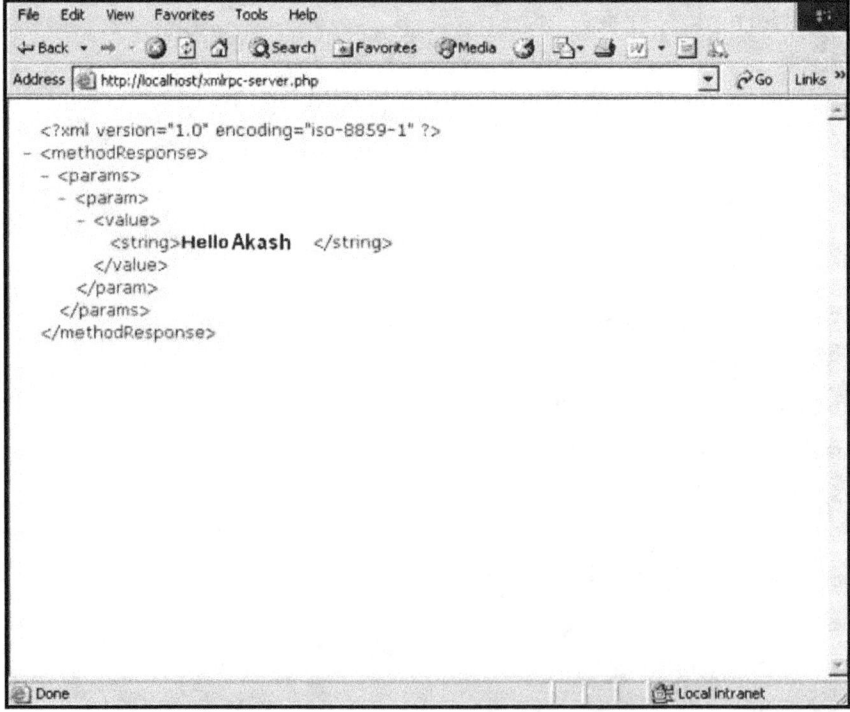

Fig. 5.12 : Response from XML-RPC web service

To demonstrate an error in the request, returned as a <fault> element in the response XML, make the request XML not valid XML. For example replace </methodCall> with <methodCall> in the $request_xml. Invoke the xmlrpc-webservice.php. The response from the server is returned as a <fault> element that consists of a struct element value, which consists of faultCode and faultString members, as shown in Fig. 5.13.

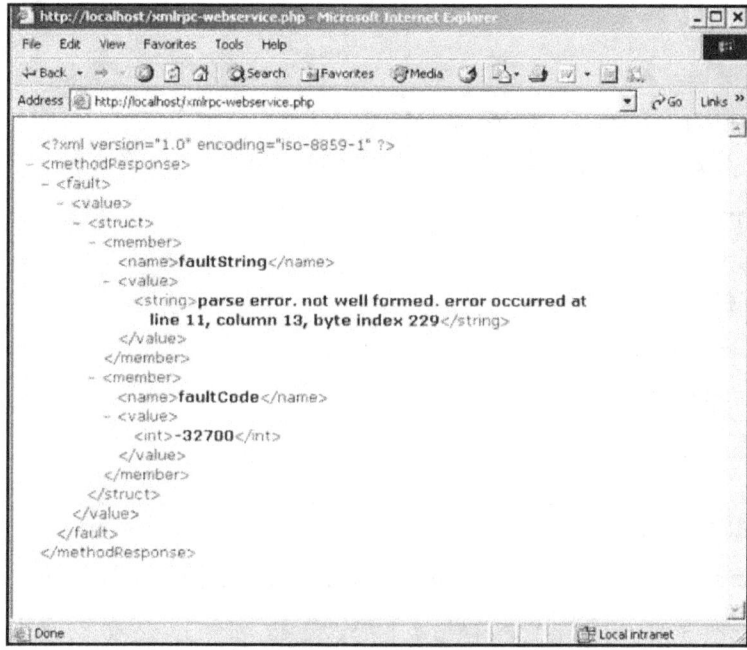

Fig. 5.13: Response as fault element

Practice Questions

1. What is Web Service ?
2. What are two categories of Web Services ?
3. What is mashup ?
4. How many ways the tools available with Web Services are used?
5. What is WSDL ?
6. Explain Web Service Architecture.
7. Explain any four elements of WSDL.
8. What is SOAP ? Explain SOAP message.
9. Wire a Note on Representation of Concepts defined by WSDL.
10. What are four basic patterns of operation supported by WSDL ?
11. Explain Soap Messaging Framework.
12. Explain structure of an XML-RPC Request.
13. What is purpose of XML-RPC ? Write any two XML-RPC PHP functions.

✍ ✍ ✍

Chapter 6...

AJAX

Contents ...

6.1 Introduction to AJAX   [April 2016, Oct. 2016]

AJAX is an acronym standing for Asynchronous JavaScript and XML. AJAX allows web pages to be update asynchronously by exchanging small amounts of data with the server behind the scenes. This means that it is possible to update parts of a web page, without reloading the whole page.

Examples of applications using AJAX:

Google Maps, Gmail, Youtube, Facebook tabs, etc.

How does AJAX work?

In an AJAX enabled application only the relevant page elements are updated, when necessary. Fig. 6.1 shows working of AJAX.

1. Initial request by the browser – the user requests the particular URL.

2. The complete page is rendered by the server (along with the JavaScript AJAX engine) and sent to the client (HTML, CSS, JavaScript AJAX engine).

3. All subsequent requests to the server are initiated as function calls to the JavaScript engine.

4. The JavaScript engine then makes an XmlHttpRequest to the server.

5. The server processes the request and sends a response in XML format to the client (XML document). It contains the data only of the page elements that need to be changed. In most cases this data comprises just a fraction of the total page markup.

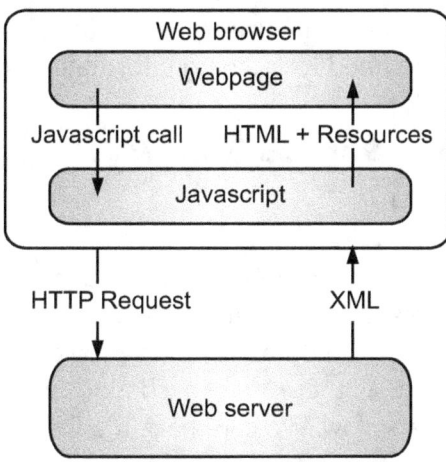

Fig. 6.1 : Working of AJAX

6. The AJAX engine processes the server response, updates the relevant page content or performs another operation with the new data received from the server, (HTML + CSS).

Advantages of AJAX

1. **Speed :** Reduce the server traffic in both side request. Also reducing the time consuming on both side response.

2. **Interaction :** AJAX is much responsive, whole page(small amount of) data transfer at a time.

3. **XMLHttpRequest :** XMLHttpRequest has an important role in the Ajax web development technique. Its is a special JavaScript object that was designed by Microsoft. XMLHttpRequest object calls as a asynchronous HTTP request to the Server for transferring data both side. It's used for making requests to the non-Ajax pages.

4. **Asynchronous calls :** AJAX make asynchronous calls to a web server. This means client browsers are avoid waiting for all data arrive before start the rendering.

5. **Form Validation :** This is the biggest advantage. Forms are common element in web page. Validation should be instant and properly, AJAX gives you all of that.

6. **Bandwidth Usage :** Bandwidth Usage no require to completely reload page again. AJAX improves the speed and performance. Fetching data from database and storing data into database perform background without reloading page.

Disadvantages of AJAX

1. AJAX application would be a mistake because search engines would not be able to index an AJAX application.

2. Open Source: View source is allowed and anyone can view the code source written for AJAX.

3. ActiveX requests are enabled only in Internet Explorer and newer latest browser.

4. For a security reason you can only use to access information from the web host that serves initial pages. If you need to fetching information from another server, it's is not possible with in the AJAX.

6.2 Understanding Java Scripts for AJAX

Introduction to Java Script

We can develop the web pages using two technologies, HTML and CGI (Common Gateway Interface). For creating dynamic web pages, the dynamic technologies are used such as asp, asp.net, php or JSP. In this, user entered some data into the forms, which is then sent to the server. The server processes the data and then provided the response to the browser in the form of HTML document. If there was, a change and whole process needs to be repeated, due to this, process gets slow. We can make it a fast process by using Java Script.

The Java script is executed by the browser on the user's computer. This type of code is called client-side code and this type of approach results in fast running web sites. Java script is an interpreted language, if it doesn't need any compiler to execute a code.

The Java scripts are also called Live Script. It is a scripting language and it is not related to Java. It is used to make the web pages interactive. We can use java script in web application on following conditions:

- **Data entry validations:** A Java script can be used to validate the data entered in the form.
- **HTML Interactivity:** Using java script, we can make web page interactive means user can get the feedback as soon as he enters the data in a form.
- **Serverless CGI's:** With java script, we can do validation on client side, which increase the performance.
- **CGI prototyping:** We can easily create a prototype of CGI in client side using java script.
- **Off-loading a busy server:** For heavy trafficked website, it is useful to convert the frequently used CGI process to the client-side java scripts.
- **Adding life to otherwise-dead pages :** Using java script, we can add some interactive zip to web page, it may engage the user and repeat visits.

Advantages of Java Script

Following are some advantages of Java Script:

1. **Less server interaction:** We can validate the user input before sending the page off to the server. Using this, we can save the server traffic that means saving money.
2. **Immediate feedback to the visitors:** The user doesn't have to wait for a page reload to see if they have forgotten to enter something.
3. **Automated fixing of minor errors:** For example, if the database system required date in the dd–mm–yyyy format and the user enter it in the dd–mm–yyyy form, a clever Java script could change this minor mistake into correct form before sending the form to the server.

4. **Increased interactivity:** We can create interfaces that react when the user brows them with a mouse or activates them via the keyboard.

5. **Richer interface:** We can use Java script to include items, such as drag and drop component and sliders.

6. **Light weight environment:** The java script uses the browser controls for functionality rather than it's own user interfaces, like flash or java applets do. This makes it easier for users, as they already know these controls.

Basics of Java Script

Syntax of java script :

Java script is case sensitive. All the java script coding is written between the opening and closing <script> tag.

e.g. Java.html   or   Java.js

→   <html>

<body>

<script type = "text/java script">

document.write ("Hello world !")

</script>

</body>

</html>

This code produce output Hello world !, the document. write is the standard java script command for writing the output to a page.

We can use // for current line as comment. The multiple line comment start with /* and end with */.

Curly braces {&} are used to indicate a block of code. The code inside the braces is treated as one block.

The semicolons are optional in java script but it is a good practice to use semicolons in the document.

Data Types in Java Scripts

Various data types in Java scripts are as follows:

1. **Number:** Used for both integer and floating point numbers.

2. **String:** For group of one or more characters.

3. **Boolean:** For True or False.

4. **Undefined:** It has only one value i.e. undefined. It use only when a variable is declared, but not assigned any value.

5. **Null:** It has only one value i.e. null. The null value means that the object in the question doesn't exist.

Variables

A variable is referred as the container for storing information. The value of a variable can change during the script. Use the var keyword followed by the name you want to give to the variable.

For example,

> Var num = 9;
>
> Var name = "Sonal";

We don't need to declare a data type.

Operators

Operators enable us to perform an action on a variable : Following are the various operators available in Java scripts :

1. Assignment operator : i.e. var a = 9;
2. Arithmetic operators : +, −, *, /, % (mod)

We can use + operator also for concatenation of two strings.

3. Comparison operator : >, <, > =, < =, ==, !=
4. Logical operators : Logical operator includes && and, !! or, ! Not
5. Increment and decrement operators :

For example,

> var a = 1;
>
> a++; //a = 2
>
> var b = 10;
>
> b − −; //b = 9

Conditional Statements and Loops

JavaScript also includes a basic set of programming statements.

- **Conditional :** if/else, switch
- **Loops :** for, while, do while.

Let us see Conditional statements :

1. If/else : The following code shows use of if/else statement in the Java script which display message,

Good morning if time is less than 12, otherwise Good Day message.

```
<script type = "text/javascript">
var d = new Date();
var time = d.getHours();
if(time<12)
{
document.write("Good Morning");
}
```

```
else
{
document.write("Good Day");
}


</script>
```

2. **Switch :** The switch statement is used in place of a series of if statements.

switch (num)

```
{
    Case 1 : execute block 1
          break;
    Case 2 : execute block 2
          break;
    default :
       Code to be executed if n is different from case 1 and 2
}
```

- **Loops :** Loops are a way to repeat a block of code based on the conditions that we specify.

1. **'for' loop :** A for loop is used when you know in advance how many times the script should run.

For example, display the number from 0 to 6.

```
<html>
<body>
<script>
var i = 0;


for (i = 0; i < 6; i++)
{
   document.write("The number is"+i);
   document.write("<br/>");
}
</script>


</body>
</html>
```

```
Output   :
           0
           1
           2
           3
           4
           5
```

2. While loop : A while loop is used when you want the loop to execute and continue executing, while the specified condition is true.

For example, display the number from 0 to 6

```html
<html>
<body>
    <script>
      var text = "";
      var i = 0;
      while (i <= 6) {
          text += "<br>The number is " + i;
          i++;
      }
      document.write(text);
    </script>

</body>
</html>
```

```
Output   0
         1
         2
         3
         4
         5
         6
```

3. do-while loop : It is a variant of the while loop. This loop will always execute a block of code once.

For example,

```html
<html>
<body>
```

```
<script type = "text/javascript">
    var text = "";
 var i = 0;
 do {
     text += "<br>The number is " + i;
     i++;
 }
 while (i <= 6)
  document.write(text);

</script>
    </body>
    </html>
    Output    0
              1
              2
              3
              4
              5
              6
```

Functions

A function is a reusable group if code statements that are treated as a unit. Function definitions are usually included in script blocks in the head section of HTML/XHTML page. A function must be defined before it can be used. Functions are usually defined in the head section and called from the body section.

For example,

```
<html>
<body>

<p>Click button</p>

<button onclick="myFunction()">Try it</button>

<p id="demo"></p>

<script>
```

```
function myFunction() {
    alert("JavaScript function");
}
</script>

</body>
</html>
```

The message will be displayed only when the user clicks on the "try" button.

The function which returns factorial of a number.

```
function factorial(num)
    {
        var fact = 1;
        var i;
        for (i = 1; i < = num; i++)
        fact = fact * i;
        return fact;
    }
```

Java Script Objects

An object is a collection of properties and methods that are grouped together with a single name. The objects available in the Javascript can be divided into three categories :

1. Built-in objects
2. Browser objects
3. User-defined objects

1. Built-in Objects

There are nine built-in objects available in Javascript. These objects are also called core language objects. The commonly used objects are Array, String, Math and Date.

Array : Using new keyword, we can create instance of the object.

For example, var obj_array = new Array( );

The obj_array has all the methods and properties of all Array Objects.

To reverse the order of members of the array :

var reverse_ary = obj_array.reverse( );

To find the length of array, 'length' property is used :

var ary_len = obj_array.length;

String : The string object is used to manipulate a stored piece of text.

var text = "PHP and Javascript";

document.write(text.length);

To convert the string into upper case :

```
var text = "php";
document.write (text.toUpper case ( ));
```

Math : This object allows you to perform common mathematical tasks. Javascript provides eight mathematical values (constants) that can be accessed from the math object. These are :

1. Math.E
2. Math.PI
3. Math.SQRT2
4. Math.SQRT1_2 : square root of 1/2
5. Math.LN2 : natural log of 2
6. Math.LN10 : natural log of 10
7. Math.LOG2E : base 2 log of E
8. Math.LOG10E : base 10 log of E

The round( ) method is used to round a number,

```
document.write (Math.round (4.7));
output = 5
```

The random ( ) method is used to generate random number between 0 to 1

```
document.write (Math.random ( ));
output = 0.4906783821253167
```

Date : This object works with date and times

```
var myDate = new Date( );
myDate.setFullYear (2010, 0, 20) //set date to 20th January 2010
var today = new Date( );
//set current date
if (myDate > today)
    alert ("Today is before 20th January 2010");
else
    alert ("Today is after 20th January 2010);
```

2. Browser Objects

The Browser Object Model (BOM) is a collection of objects that interact with the browser window.

Window :

- Screen
- Navigator
- Document

- History
- Location

To display message, use alert function, also we can write this function as window.alert ("Look ! is there a reference");

The history object keeps track of every page the user visits. It include forward, back and go.

> history.back (2); //go back 2 by pages.

The location object contains the URL of the page. We can use href property to go to a new page

> location.href = "mypage.html";

At the top of the object hierarchy is the window object. A window object method enables you to create a separate window that appears on screen.

> window.methodName (parameters);

A widow object also has a synonym. We replace the window object by its synonym self.

> self.methodName (Parameters);

The method generates the new window window.open(). It contains upto three parameters, which will define the characteristics, such as the URL of the document to load, its name for the target attribute, reference purpose in HTML tags and the physical appearance.

For example,

> var subwindows = window.open ("definition.html", "def", "height = 225, width = 400");

For closing this window, close( ) method is used

> subwindow.close ( );

1. The alert( ) method generates a dialog box that displays the text that is passed as a parameter. A single OK button enables the user to dismiss the alert.
2. The confirm( ) method that returns the value : true if user click OK and false if user click cancel button.
3. The prompt( ) method display dialog box, that we set and provides a text field for entering the user's response.
4. The print( ) method is used to print the contents of the current windows. e.g. window.print( );
5. The prompt( ) method display a dialog box that prompts the user for input. For example, prompt (text, default text)

The location object represents the URL loaded into the windows.

The properties of location objects are host, hostname, href, pathname, protocol. The methods available with this are assign( ), reload( ) and replace( ).

The navigator object : The navigator object is implemented in almost every scriptable browser. The navigator.userAgent property returns a string with a number of details about the browser and the operating system.

The document object : It holds the real contents of the page. Properties and methods of the document generally affect the look and content of the document that occupies the window.

For example, window.document.methodName (parameter).

Methods like, write( ), open( ), close( ), anchors( ), forms( ), images( ), links( ) are available.

The history object : The browser maintain a list of URL, for most recent stops. This list is represented in the scriptable object model by the history object. The methods like back( ), forward( ) and go( ) are available.

The screen object : This is read only object in that the script learn about the physical environment in which the browser is running. The methods are availHeight, availWidth, bufferDepth, height, width.

For example, screen.width

3. **User-Defined Object**

All user-defined objects and built-in objects are ancestors of an object called Object.

The New Operator

The new operator is used to create an instance of an object. To create an object, the new operator is followed by the constructor method.

In the following example, the constructor methods are Object(), Array(), and Date(). These constructors are built-in JavaScript functions.

```
var employee = new Object();
var books = new Array("C++", "Perl", "Java");
var day = new Date("August 15, 1947");
```

The Object() Constructor

A constructor is a function that creates and initializes an object. JavaScript provides a special constructor function called **Object()** to build the object. The return value of the **Object()** constructor is assigned to a variable.

The variable contains a reference to the new object. The properties assigned to the object are not variables and are not defined with the **var** keyword.

Example 1

Try the following example; it demonstrates how to create an Object.

```
<html>
   <head>
      <title>User-defined objects</title>
```

```
<script type="text/javascript">
   var book = new Object();    // Create the object
   book.subject = "Perl"; // Assign properties to the object
   book.author  = "Mohtashim";
</script>


</head>

<body>


<script type="text/javascript">
   document.write("Book name is : " + book.subject + "<br>");
   document.write("Book author is : " + book.author + "<br>");
</script>


</body>
</html>
```

Output

```
Book name is : Perl
Book author is : Mohtashim
```

Document Object Model (DOM)

It is tree based representation of a document. The DOM was created by the World Wide Web Consortium (W3C) for XML and HTML/XHTML. It is divided into following three parts :

The Core Dom, it includes objects which are common in XML and HTML.

The XML DOM includes the XML objects.

The HTML DOM includes the HTML objects.

The document can be viewed as a node tree. There are several types of nodes, but main nodes are Element nodes and Text node.

The node type property returns the type of node :

Table 6.1

Node Type	Element Type
1	Element
2	Attribute
3	Text
8	Comment
9	Document

There are two methods available in DOM for accessing various elements of the document :

1. **getElementById( ) :** It returns the element with the specified ID.

    Syntax : document.getElementById ("Id");

    e.g. : document.getElementById ('el').parentNode;

It will access parent node of the head and body elements.

    document.getElementById ('e2').childNodes;

It will access all the children of the body element.

2. **getElementsByTagName( ) :** This method returns all elements with the specified tag name that are descendants of the element.

    document.getElementById ('Id').getElementsByTagName ("tagnames");

                                OR

    document.getElementsByTagName ("tagname");

The W3C DOM specifications are divided into levels.

1. **Level 0 :** Application supports an intermediate DOM.

2. **Level 1 :** It includes the navigation of DOM (HTML an XML) document.

3. **Level 2 :** XML namespace support, filtered views and events.

4. **Level 3 :** It consists of six different specifications. These are,

DOM level 3 Core, DOM level 3 load and save, DOM level 3 XPath, DOM level 3 views and formatting, DOM level 3 Requirements and DOM level 3 validation

Simple javascript program which check the number is Armstrong number.

```
<html>
<head><TITLE> Armstrong Number </TITLE>
<script language="JavaScript">
var b,tmp,total=0;
var a=prompt("Enter a number");
tmp=a;
while(tmp>0)
{
b=tmp%10;
total=total+(b*b*b);
tmp=parseInt(tmp/10);
}
if(a==total)
alert("given no is amstrong number");
else
alert("given no is not an amstrong number");
```

```
</script>
</head>
<body></body>
</html>
```

Javascript is very useful in the AJAX technique. Using AJAX, the javascript can communicate directly with the server, using the Javascript object which directly handle the data without reloading the page. AJAX uses asynchronous data transfer (HTTP requests) between the browser and the webserver, it allows web page to request small bits of information from the server, instead of whole pages. The AJAX technique makes internet application smaller, faster and more user friendly.

Creating a Java Script Application with AJAX

In this application, we will implement how javascript uses the XML HTTPRrequest object for sending the request to the server and receiving response from the server. The application start with HTML page, Index.html that display a button labeled change content.

This application shows the effect of AJAX and also without AJAX.

Index.html

```
<html>
<head>
<meta http-equiv="Content-Type" content=''text/html;
charset=iso-8859-1''>
<title>Ajax Demo</title>
<script type=''text/javascript''>
function loadXMLDoc()
{
if (window.XMLHttpRequest)
   {//code for IE7+, Firefox, Chrome, Opera, Safari
   xmlhttp=new XMLHttpRequest();
   }
else
   {//code for IE6, IE5
   xmlhttp=new ActiveXObject(''Microsoft.XMLHTTP'');
   }
xmlhttp.onreadystatechange=function()
   {
   if (xmlhttp.readyState==4 && xmlhttp.status==200)
       {
document.getElementById(''myDiv'').innerHTML=xmlhttp.response Text;
       }
   }
```

```
xmlhttp.open(''GET'', ''ajax_report.php'',true);
xmlhttp.send();
}
</script>
</head>
<body>
<div id=''myDiv''><h2>Let AJAX change this text</h2>
      <button type=''button'' onclick=''loadXMLDoc()''>Change Content
</button>
</div>
<div><h2>Let without AJAX change this text</h2>
      <a href=''new_text.php''><button type=''button''>Change Content
</button></a>
</div>
</body>
</html>
```

new_text.php
```
<html>
<head>
<meta http-equiv=''Content-Type'' Content=''text/html;
charset=iso-8859-1''>
<title>Without Ajax</title>
</head>
<body>
<div  id=''myDiv''><div>
      <h1>This is Ajax Test</h1>
      <p>
            AJAX is not a new programming language.<br>
            AJAX is a technique for creating fast and dynamic
web pages.
      </p>
</div>
</body>
</html>
```
ajax_report.php
```
<div>
      <h1>This is Ajax Test</h1>
      <p>
         AJAX is not a new programming language.<br>
         AJAX is a technique for creating fast and dynamic web
pages.
      </p>
</div>
```

6.3 AJAX Web Application Model   [April 2016]

AJAX uses Javascript and XML as the main technology for developing interactive web applications. These applications are based on AJAX web application model, which uses JavaScript and XMLHTTPRequest object for asynchronous data exchange.

The problem with classical web application model is slow, that was resolved through AJAX. The AJAX application eradicates the start-stop-start-stop nature or the click, wait and refresh criteria of the client-server interaction.

The Fig. 6.1 shows how the new layer is introduced between the user and the web server.

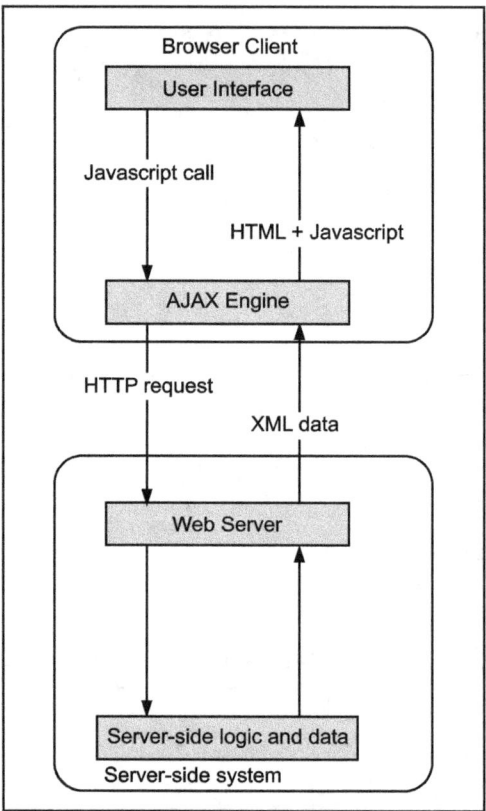

Fig. 6.2 : AJAX Web application model

The browser loads the ajax engine, which is written in JavaScript at the beginning of the web page. This JavaScript makes a request to the server. The server response includes data and not the presentation, which implies that the data required by the page is provided by the server as the response and with the help of markup language style or presentation is implemented. Due to this, most of the page does not change; this means that small part of the page that needs to change and updated. This is done dynamically without displaying everything again. This way, we never have to wait for updations. This is the power of asynchronous request. The AJAX engine takes care of displaying the user interface and the interaction with the server. It uses XMLHttpRequest object for the communication. The XMLHttpRequest object has the property named onreadystatechange, which allows handling the asynchronous loading operations. If this property is assigned to the name of any javascript function, then this function will be called each time the XMLHttpRequest object's state changes,

xmlhttp.onreadystatechange = function( )

This function is also known as "callback" function. When the server returns with the information, the callback function is invoked. When the XMLHttpRequest object is in its ready state and the status is equal to 200, then data is fetched. The readystate value "4" indicates that the request is completed and the status 200 refers to the "OK" state of the XMLHttpRequest object, this means that the request resource is completely downloaded.

The XMLHttpRequest object has five ready states. These are :

Table 6.2

State	Description
0	Uninitialized state
1	Loading state
2	Loaded state
3	Interactive state
4	The complete state

Some possible values for the status property of XMLHttpRequest object.

Table 6.3

Value	Status	Value	Status
200	OK	408	Request timeout
201	Created	411	Length required
204	No content	413	Requested entry too large
205	Reset content	414	Requested URL too long
206	Partial content	415	Unsupport media type
400	Bad request	500	Internal server error
401	Unauthorised status	501	Not implemented
403	Forbidden status	502	Bad gateway
404	Not found status	503	Server unavailable
405	Method not allowed	504	Gateway time out
406	Not acceptable	505	HTTP version not supported
407	Proxy Authentication Required		

6.4 AJAX-PHP Framework

The PHP-frameworks gives different ways to affect the client view in both template based view (uses technologies like JSP, ASP and RHTML) and server-side technologies (like ASP.NET and JSP).

This functionality becomes popular in the server side AJAX packages, because it automatically create JavaScript code for us.

There are various PHP frameworks available, like AJAXCore, CakePHP, Xajax, Sajax, XOAD, Zephyr, Feather AJAX 1.1 and Tigermouse to integrate AJAX with PHP. These frameworks supports Model, View and Controller (MVC) architecture. They reduces the writing of same code and common function repeatedly.

The Sajax is an AJAX based framework, which generate AJAX-enabled JavaScript from many server side languages like PHP, ASP, ColdFusion, Io, Lua, Perl, Python and Ruby. This Sajax bridge execute server side code and uses Object Remoting technique. The object brokers enable remote exchange and the client-side methods are tied to the server side object. There are network round trips involved and messages are sent via service oriented frameworks.

Sajax framework example:

In this example, JavaScript function generates from PHP function on server side that manipulates data and returns result to other JavaScript function on client side.

The Home page of mult.php has three text fields where user can enter two numbers in first two text field and in third text field, result is displayed. There is one submit button in home page. We have to include Sajax.php in mult.php. We need to setup Sajax using Sajax_init ( ) method. This file contains function mult for multiplication of two numbers. To access this function in JavaScript by another name, we need to export this method, like x_mult.

The part of mult.php :

```
<?
    require ("Sajax.php");
    function mult ($no1, $no2)
    {
        return $no1 * $no2;
    }
    Sajax_init ();
    Sajax_export ("mult");
    Sajax_handle_client_request ();
    //it connect mult function with Sajax and generate JavaScript ?>
```

The generated JavaScript code can be embed in web page using PHP function Sajax_show_javascript ( );

After Clicking on Submit button, it invokes x_mult function, which in turn calls mult function on server side.

The part of mult.php :

```
<script>
<?
Sajax_show_javascript ();
?>
function show_results (result)
{
    docment.getElementById ("result").value=result;
}
function do_add()
{
    var no1, no2;
    no1 = document.getElementById ("No1").value;
    no2 = document.getElementById ("No2").value;
    x_mult (no1, no2, show_results);
}
</script>
```

The x_mult uses three argument, first is value, second is value and third is a function name which will display the result of multiplication.

6.5 Performing AJAX Validation

The validation may done for checking integer, email id or phone number etc. The first page for application displays the text field to enter the username. It has JavaScript code to create the XMLHttpRequest object. The validate method sends request to validate the PHP page with parameter name.

When status of response is OK, the <div> element having id res, is populated with the text response received from server. When new request comes in the abort, method exists from the previous request.

Ajax.html

```
<script type=''text/javascript''>
var http = false;
if(navigator.appName == ''Microsoft Internet Explorer'')
{
    http = new ActiveXObject (''Microsoft.XMLHTTP'');
}
```

```
else  {
        http = new XMLHttpRequest();
    }
function validate (name)
   {
   http.abort();
   http.open(''GET'', ''Validate.php?name='' + name, true);
   http.onreadystatechange=function()
      {
       if(http.readyState == 4)
       {
    document.getElementById('res').innerHTML = http.responseText;
       }
    }
   http.send(null);
}
</script>
<h1>Type username to choose:</h1>
<form>
    <input type=''text'' name=''name'' onkeyup=''validate(this.value)''/>
    <div id=''res''></div>
</form>
```

The Ajax.html and validate.php files are stored into html directory and executed in browser.

```
        http://localhost/Ajax.html
```

The Ajax.html file calls validate.php where validation is done. If name is blank or name is less than 3 characters or if name is already exists, the corresponding messages are given.

validate.php

```php
<?php
function validate ($name)
   {
       if($name =='')
       {
           return 'Please enter any username';
       }
       if(strlen($name) < 3)
```

```php
    {
        return ''Username is too short.'';
    }
  switch($name)
    {
        case 'Anu':
        case 'Jyoti':
        case 'Meena':
        case 'Sonal':
            return "Username already exists.";
    }
    return "Username is valid.";
}
echo validate(trim($_REQUEST["name"]));
?>
```

6.6 Handling XML Data using PHP and AJAX   [Oct. 2016]

XML files are used to store data using our own defined tags. The following example shows how to get the data from XML file using AJAX. The index.html file use choosebook.js JavaScript file. This form shows the Book title to the user and when user select the title from list box, the sendTitle method from choosebook.js is called.

index.html

```html
<html>
<head>
<script src=''choosebook.js''></script>
</head><body><form>
List of Book Title :
<selectname=''titles''onchange=''sendTitle(this.value)''>
<option>Select a Book Title</option>
<option value=''PHP''>PHP</option>
<option value=''JAVA''>JAVA</option>
<option value=''ASP''>ASP</option>
</select>
</form><p>
<div id=''res''><b>Book Information will be given here.</b></div>
</p></body>
</html>
```

The booksdata.xml file stores the Book's details like Title, Author, Year and price sub elements.

booksdata.xml

```xml
<?xml version=''1.0'' encoding=''ISO-8859-1''?>
<Bookdata>
<Book>
<Title>PHP</Title>
<Author>Akash</Author>
<Year>2010</Year>
<Price>80.00</Price>
</Book>
<Book>
<Title>JAVA</Title>
<Author>Santosh</Author>
<Year>2009</Year>
<Price>130.00</Price>
</Book>
<Title>ASP</Title>
<Author>Vilas</Author>
<Year>2008</Year>
<Price>210.00</Price>
</Book>
<Book>
<Title>JSP</Title>
<Author>Rajesh</Author>
<Year>2010</Year>
<Price>320.00</Price>
</Book>
</Bookdata>
```

The GetXmlHttpObject() method create URL to request getbook.php file. This URL has parameter q which is used to initialize the value of list box, then sends the request to getbook.php page. After completion of response by the server, the stateChanged method is called.

Code for Javascript file :

choosebook.js

```
var xmlHttp;
```

```
function sendTitle(str)
{
xmlHttp=GetXmlHttpObject();
if(xmlHttp==null)
    {
    alert(''Browser does not support HTTP Request'');
    return;
    }
var url=''getbook.php'';
url=url+''?q=''+str;
xmlHttp.onreadystatechange=stateChanged;
xmlHttp.open(''GET'',url,true)
xmlHttp.send(null)
}
function stateChanged()
    {
        if(xmlHttp.readyState==4||xmlHttp.readyState=''complete'')
        {
    document.getElementById(''res'').innerHTML=xmlHttp.responseText;
        }
    }
    function GetXmlHttpObject()
    {
    varxmlHttp=null;
try{
        //for Firefox,
        xmlHttp=new XMLHttpRequest();
        }
    catch(e)
    {
    //for Internet Explorer
    try
        {
        xmlHttp=new ActiveXObject(''Msxml2.XMLHTTP'');
        }
    catch(e)
```

```
        {
        xmlHttp=new ActiveXObject(''Microsoft.XMLHTTP'');
        }
    return xmlHttp;
}
```

The server page getbook.php create XML DOMDocument object user select an Option. Then booksdata.xml file is loaded. The Title send from HTML form search in booksdata.xml file. Thisway the correct title is found.

getbook.php

```php
<?php
$q=$_GET(''q'');
$xmlDoc = new DOMDocument();
$xmlDoc->load(''booksdata.xml'')'
$x=$xmlDoc->getElementsByTagName('Title');
for($i=0; $i<=$x->length-1;$i++)
{
//Process only element nodes
if ($x->item($i)->nodeType==1)
    {
    if ($x->item($i)->childNodes->item(0)->nodeValue == $q)
        {
        $y=($x->item($i)->parentNode);
        }
    }
}$book=($y->childNodes);
for($i=0;$i<$book->length,$i++)
{
//Process only element nodes
if ($book->?item($i)->nodeType==1)
    {
    echo($book->item($i)->nodeName);
    echo('':'');
    echo($book->item($i)->childNodes->item(0)-nodeValue);
    echo(''<br/>'');
    }
}
?>
```

We can execute this application http://localhost.index.html

6.7 Connecting Database using PHP and AJAX

Storing the data and retrieving it, we can do using PHP and MYSQL. Consider an example of employee database table. From index.html form, we can select the employee name using combo box and display its record details.

Create 'Employees' Database in MYSQL, the table 'emprecord' having fields Name, Age, City, Designation. Insert the names as per index.html with all details.

index.html

```
<html>
<head>
<script src=''ajax.js''></script>
</head>
<body><form>
Employees Title:
<selectname=''names''onchange=''sendEmpID(this.value)''>
<option>Select Name</option>
<option value=''1''>Mahesh</option>
<option value=''2''>Sachin</option>
<option value=''3''>Tejas</option>
<option value=''4''>Bhavesh</option>
<option value=''5''>Amit</option>
</select>
</form><p>
<div id=''emp''><b>Book Info will be listed here.</b></div>
</p></body>
</html>
```

The method sendEmpID calls the GetXmlHttpObject, which takes asynchronous request to getemployee.php file. The request URL has parameter q to store id and sid to store random numbers in order to avoid the server from taking the cached file. It send the request to getemployee.php with parameter.

ajax.js

```
var xmlHttp;
function sendEmpID(str)
{
xmlHttp=GetXmlHttpObject();
if(xmlHttp==null)
    {
    alert(''HTTP Request not supported by browser'')
    return;
    }
var url=''getemployee.php'';
url=url+''?q=''str;
url=url+''&sid=''+Math.random();
xmlHttp.onreadystatechange=stateChanged;
xmlHttp.open(''GET'',url,true);
xmlHttp.send(null);
}
function stateChanged()
    {
        if(xmlHttp.readyState==4||xmlHttp.readyState=''complete'')
        {
     document.getElementById(''emp'').innerHTML=xmlHttp.responseText;
        }
    }
    function GetXmlHttpObject()
    {
    varxmlHttp=null;
    try
        {
        //Firefox, Opera 8.0+, Safari
        xmlHttp=new XMLHttpRequest();
        }
```

```
catch(e)
{
//Internet Explorer
try
    {
    xmlHttp=new ActiveXObject(''Msxml2.XMLHTTP'');
    }
catch(e)
    {
    xmlHttp=new ActiveXObject(''Microsoft.XMLHTTP'');
}
returnxmlHttp;
}
```

After selecting the employee name, it sends the id as query parameter to getemployee.php page, this page establish the connection to MYSQL server by using user id root and password root. Change the Id and Password what you have. After successful connection, it will retrieve data and using HTML table, the fetched values are inserted into corresponding cell or row.

getemployee.php.

```
<?php
$q=$_GET(''q'');
$con = mysql_connect('localhost', 'root', 'root');
if (!$con)
    {
    die('Not able to connect: ' . mysql_error());
    }
mysql_select_db(''employees'', $con);
$query=''SELECT'' * FROM emprecord WHERE id = ' ''.$q.'' ' '';
$result = mysql_query($query);
echo ''<table border='1'>
<tr>
<th>Name</th>
```

```
<th>Age</th>
<th>City</th>
<th>Designation</th>
</tr>'';
while($row = mysql_fetch_array($result))
    {
    echo ''<tr>'';
    echo ''<tr>''; . $row['name'] . ''</td>'';
    echo ''<tr>''; . $row['age'] . ''</td>'';
    echo ''<tr>''; . $row['city'] . ''</td>'';
    echo ''<tr>''; . $row['designation'] . ''</td>'';
    echo ''<tr>'';
    }
echo ''</table>'';
mysql_close($con);
?>
```

We execute this using http://localhost index.html

Practice Questions

(I) Answer in short:

1. What is Ajax?

2. How we make web page interactive?

3. True/False - Java script is an interpreted language.

4. What is the Java Script Object?

5. What is use of 'alert' method?

6. True/False - The Screen Object are Read-Only Object.

7. What are the different methods in history Object?

8. What is the use of XMLHttpRequest ?

9. What is the callback function?

10. What is meaning of XMLHttpRequest ready state value is 4?

(II) Answer the following questions:

1. Explain the merits of JavaScript.

2. What are different conditions where JavaScript can be used?

3. Explain different Data types in JavaScript.

4. Write a JavaScript to display the message if time is less than 12 display good morning otherwise display good afternoon.

5. Explain Browser Object in JavaScript.

6. What is DOM? Explain getElementById ( ).

7. Write a code using JavaScript for implementation to Ajax.

UNIVERSITY QUESTION PAPERS
APRIL 2016

Time : 3 Hours   **Max. Marks : 80**

N.B.:   (i)   *All questions are compulsory.*

          (ii)   *Figures are required whenever necessary.*

1. Attempt the following (any eight) :   **[16]**

   (a)   What is Introspection ?

Ans.   Refer Section 1.4.

   (b)   Enlist the name of functions to extract basic information about classes in PHP.

Ans.   Refer Section 4.3.

   (c)   Enlist the HTTP Request Methods.

Ans.   Refer Section 6.1 Advantages of Ajax.

   (d)   What is $-SERVER ?

Ans.   Refer Section 2.2.

   (e)   Which are the databases supported by PHP ?

Ans.   Refer Section 4.3.

   (f)   Enlist the methods of PEAR DB ?

Ans.   Refer Section 3.5.

   (g)   What is XML ?

Ans.   Refer Section 4.1.

   (h)   Enlist the predefined internal entities in XML.

Ans.   Refer Section 4.2.

   (i)   What is WSDL ?

Ans.   Refer Section 5.2.

   (j)   What is XML HTTP Request ?

Ans.   Refer Section 6.1.

2. Attempt the following (any four) :   **[16]**

   (a)   Define Constructor. Explain with the help of program.

Ans.   Refer Section 1.3.

   (b)   What is Self-Processing Form ? Explain with the help of program.

Ans.   Refer Section 2.4.

   (c)   What is Database ? Explain different functions in PhP to connect to the MySql.

Ans.   Refer Section 3.2.

   (d)   Create student table as follows :

           student (Sno, Sname, Per).

      Write Ajax Program to select the student name and print the selected students details.

Ans.   Refer Programs in Chapter 6.

   (e)   Write PHP script to create a CD catalog using XML file. (CD catalogue includes - Title, Author and Price).

Ans.   Refer Programs in Chapter 4.

3. Attempt the following (any four) :   [16]
(a) Explain XML document structure.
Ans. Refer Section 4.2.
(b) Explain classical web application model and Ajax web application model.
Ans. Refer Section 6.3.
(c) Write a PHP script to demonstrate the introspection for examining class (use function get-declared-classes( ) get-class-methods( ) and get-class-vars( ).
Ans. Refer Programs in Section 1.4.
(d) Change the preferences of your web page like font style, font size, font colour, background colour using cookie. Display selected new settings) on third web page.
Ans. Refer Programs in Section 2.6.
(e) Write a PHP script to accept student details (rno, name, class) and store them in student table (Max 10), print them in sorted order of name on the browser in table format.
Ans. Refer Programs in Section 3.2.

4. Attempt the following (any four) :   [16]
(a) How to examine objects ? Explain it with the help of example.
Ans. Refer Section 1.3.
(b) What is Cookie ? List the different parts of it.
Ans. Refer Section 2.6.
(c) Explain the fetching of result from a query with the help of example.
Ans. Refer Section 3.3.
(d) Write PHP program to select list of subjects and (use multivalved parameter) displays on next page.
Ans. Refer Programs in Chapter 2.
(e) Write a PHP program to accept two string from user and check whether entered strings are matching or not.
Ans. Refer Programs in Chapter 1.

5. Write short notes on (any four) :   [16]
(a) Redirection.
Ans. Refer Section 2.5.1.1.
(b) Destructor.
Ans. Refer Section 1.3.
(c) File upload.
Ans. Refer Section 2.4.7.
(d) XML parser.
Ans. Refer Section 4.4.
(e) SOAP.
Ans. Refer Section 5.3.

OCTOBER 2016

Time : 3 Hours   Max. Marks : 80

N.B.: (i) All questions are compulsory.

(ii) Figures are required whenever necessary.

1. Attempt the following (any eight) :   [16]

(a) What is XML ?

Ans. Refer Section 4.1.

(b) What is UDDI ?

Ans. Refer Section 5.2.

(c) What is $-SERVER ?

Ans. Refer Section 2.3.

(d) What is PEARDB ?

Ans. Refer Section 3.5.

(e) Which are the databases supported by PHP ?

Ans. Refer Section 4.3.

(f) Enlist the global variables in PHP.

Ans. Refer Section 2.2.

(g) What is XMLHttpRequest ?

Ans. Refer Section 6.1.

(h) What is Serialization ?

Ans. Refer Section 1.5.

(i) Enlist the predefined internal entities in XML ?

Ans. Refer Section 4.2.

(j) Enlist the elements of XML document.

Ans. Refer Section 4.1.

2. Attempt the following (any four) :   [16]

(a) Explain how to create and select database using PHP.

Ans. Refer Section 3.2.

(b) Define constructor. Explain it with the help of program.

Ans. Refer Section 1.3.

(c) What are the response header ? Give various ways for setting response header.

Ans. Refer Section 2.5.

(d) Write a PHP script to create a CD catalog using XML File.

Ans. Refer Section 4.????

(e) Write a program, create Bus table as follows :
Bus (bno, bname, source, designation).
Write AJAX program to select bus name and print the selected bus details.

Ans. Refer Section 6.6.

3. Attempt the following (any four) :   [16]

(a) Explain the need of web services.

Ans. Refer Section 5.1.

(b) Explain XML document structure.

Ans. Refer Section 4.2.

(c) Define an interface which has methods area( ), volume( ). Define constant PI. Create a class cylinder which implements this interface and calculate area and volume (use defined ( )).

Ans. Refer Section 1.7.

(d) Write PHP script to accept student details (rno, name, class) and store them in student table (Max 10). Print them in sorted order of name on the browser in table format.

Ans. Refer Section 3.7.

(e) Create a login form with a username and password. Once the user logs in, the second form should be displayed to accept user details enter information within a specified time limit, expire his session and give a warning otherwise display details ($-SESSION).

Ans. Refer Section 2.6.

4. Attempt the following (any four) :   [16]

(a) How to examine object ? Explain it with the help of example.

Ans. Refer Section 1.3.

(b) What is Session ? Explain with the help of suitable program.

Ans. Refer Section 2.6.

(c) Explain the fetching of result from a query with the help of example.

Ans. Refer Section 3.5.

(d) Write a PHP program to upload the file and display its information (use $-FILES).

Ans. Refer Section 2.4.7.

(e) Write a PHP program to accept two string from user and check whether entered strings are matching or not (use sticky form concept).

Ans. Refer Section 2.4.5.

5. Write short notes on (any four) :   [16]

(a) Redirection.

Ans. Refer Section 2.5.1.1.

(b) Constructor.

Ans. Refer Section 1.3.

(c) XML Parser.

Ans. Refer Section 4.4.

(d) XML RPC.

Ans. Refer Page 5.18.

(e) SOAP.

Ans. Refer Section 5.3.

✍ ✍ ✍